MW01125133

Shadows of
WAR

Jacob Lawrence Krapfl

Cover Photo: Robert Sean Evans

Copyright © 2009 Jacob Lawrence Krapfl
All rights reserved.
ISBN: 1-4392-6107-5
ISBN-13: 9781439261071
Visit www.booksurge.com to order additional copies.

For the men and women of the United States Armed Services
who shoulder the true cost of war.

For the paratroopers of
C BTRY 2/319th AFAR, 82nd ABN DIV.

For my family, my wife, and our three children.

For those mentioned here, and those who are never forgotten,
may our children learn from the blood we have shed together,
so maybe they will not have to live in the shadows of war.

Chapter One

The lighter felt almost as heavy and cold as the body armor wrapped around Sergeant Joe Busch's chest. He rolled the Miami cigarette between the fingers of his left hand savoring the almost painful need to smoke while his mind replayed the events of the patrol he just led through the center of Baghdad. Joe continued to roll the smoke gently as he brought it up under his nose to smell the Iraqi tobacco.

The chin strap to his ballistic helmet swung back and forth, caressing the left side of his jaw. He turned his head, watching a line of tracers rising out of the city five blocks away. The red balls of lead raced into the black and disappeared into the stars with their luminescent tips burned off.

Joe pinched the smoke between his lips and picked up the lighter. He sucked in the first breath of smoldering air and felt the raw refreshment deep in his lungs as he held his breath in and slowly let it trail out his nose before his mind shattered...

"Holy fuck! Get down! Now!" The faces blurred like the buildings with hallowed eye sockets for windows and mouths like skeletons. . . flashes blinked out of its nose. His men searched for cover on the trash-strewn street. The only available cover was behind a horseless produce cart. The closed mouths of houses that lined both sides of the street watched the eight men frantically dive into the debris. They returned suppressive fire in order to buy time to find better positions.

Men's shadows ran across the street in American uniforms while the eyes and noses of abandoned businesses blinked their deadly sparks. Pieces of pavement and corners of shops flew apart in explosions around the squad. Men spoke in voices clearer than the pop and zip of bullets flying around. One moaned, wounded. Joe knew who it was and tried to see his buddy's face while it stared at death, which a dying soldier sees before he dies.

Joe looked to his right. His friend and buddy since basic training lay on the street. Blood spurted a red fountain of life from his neck. His legs drew up and kicked while his fingers played hell with the blood jetting from his neck. Joe crawled over to him. He tried to look through the haze of memory into the face that wouldn't show itself but screamed Joe's name. He yelled to not let him lie like this in the street. "Don't let me die here in the middle of the street, Bro! Not like this, man. Not like this..."

"I promise, Nick. I won't let you die here, Buddy. Hang in there," Joe said comforting his buddy. Busch pulled his buddy's hand away from the neck wound only to get hit in the face with his friend's spurting blood. Wiping his face with the sleeve of his uniform, he screamed over the noise, "I gotta' put my fingers in your neck. Gotta' stop this bleeding."

He felt the heat of the body as he slipped two fingers into the gaping wound, again diverting the jets and splattering blood on his armor. The man's pulse weakly pounded against the tips of his fingers, and Joe watched as the flow slowed to a trickle. He hoped against hope that there would be enough blood still in his buddy to keep him alive as the shadowy face of death began to materialize.

"Joe...I don't want to go like this. Please...not like this... Joe. I'm sorry. I'm so sorry," PFC Nicholas Ford whispered, dying with his buddy's fingers in his neck. Joe felt the last beat of blood before his fingers began burning from what felt like breaking the ultimate promise a man can make.

"Shit! That's hot!" Joe exclaimed, snapping out of the flashback of holding his buddy through his last moments with his own fingers being burnt by a just-lit cigarette.

Still tender from the red hot cigarette, Joe flicked the smoke over the railing and watched it sail through the dark sky. He pulled open the Velcro that held his body armor together over his chest. He took a deep breath without the extra twenty-three pounds of ceramic plate and magazines full of lead. His hand found the flap over the cargo pocket on his right leg and pulled out the pack of Miami's. He smiled when he recalled the kid he bought the smokes from, a young Iraqi boy who skipped school to sell cigarettes.

"Ballsy little bastard..." he said aloud, lit another cigarette, and pocketed the smokes and lighter before raising himself out of the deckchair.

After sliding open the door into his hotel room, he stopped at the foot of his bed, took off his helmet, and dropped it to the floor. He slowly unlaced his boots and was interrupted by a loud knock on his door before he was able to kick the boots off.

He trudged over to the door of his room with his boots unlaced, body armor hanging open, and a lit cigarette that needed to be ashed dangling from his lips. He grabbed his weapon from the coat tree in the foyer and lightly gripped the handle before opening the door into a supposedly secure hallway.

"Mail, *mofo*!" Specialist Adrian Marius called out when Joe barely cracked open the door. Marius barged in.

"Oh, gee...yay, mail. Who's it from?"

"Who said any of it's for you?"

Joe turned and followed his black soldier into the room and sidetracked into the bathroom to ash his cigarette in the toilet. "You come barging into my room yelling 'Mail motherfucker!' at this time of the night, and now you're saying that you don't have any mail for me. This is bullshit. You know that you're lucky that I didn't butt-stroke your black ass in the face when you barged in here?"

"What's up with the racism? You of all people should know that I am not completely black."

"That half Jamaican almost cancels out the blackness of your mom. Almost man. Speaking of Jamaica, any chance you got any of that special grass your cousins grow so well?"

"Yeah, I have a whole kilo shoved up my black ass, and it's your job to start kissing it out, Sergeant!" Marius began to start sorting through the mail and dropping letters on the bed of Joe's roommate, Greg Forrester.

"Dude, knock off the Sergeant crap. You know you only gotta' call me that when other people are around," Joe half-ordered his trooper. Marius had outranked Busch when he got to the unit, but Joe was promoted before Marius did.

"Ahh, yes, the ways of the Army, promote the new, white kid from Iowa before the better black guy from Pennsylvania. I'm still pissed about that, ya' know."

"If that black man from Pennsylvania could run and lose that twenty pounds around his middle, he would've had his stripes a long time ago. Besides, everyone knows I'm better looking." Busch laughed and propped his weapon against the foot locker at the base of his bed and sat down to kick his canvas boots off.

"Yep, no mail for the mofo'in' white kid. Sucks to be you, man. Do you have any to be dropped off when I go back up to command?"

"Nah, I haven't had any time to write anything lately. I should probably crank out a note to Sara."

"Things going okay with the homey sweetheart?"

"Yeah, I think so." Busch didn't want to tell Marius that he thought he was falling in love with the brunette beauty from his hometown. Even some things are meant to remain private, he thought, while letting himself crack a tired smile at the thought of her.

"Whoa there, Sergeant, I see that smile..."

"Yeah, what about it?"

Marius smirked at his Sergeant and sat down next to him on the bed. "Look, Sergeant Busch. I have been in your shoes before, and I know that smile. And in my own personal opinion, you're hiding something. Your little, black buddy wants that shared before he continues on his mail rounds. Yessir, something very important..."

Joe shoved Marius in the shoulder and watched him tumble off the edge of the bed. He started to chuckle, "And in your expert opinion, what would I ever be hiding from you? Speak quickly. I'm tired and need to get some sleep." He wrapped his armor draping it around his weapon leaning against the footlocker.

"I think you're in love, Sergeant. And I think you should really tell me about this sweet piece of American pie you have waiting for you back home."

"I think you should get going on your mail runs before I start taking my pants off to get some shut eye."

"Okay. Okay. I get the idea. But before I go, I expect to see a letter written to your Sara girl tomorrow."

"Marius...you tell anyone, and I will make sure that you get stuck on every shitty detail I can think of."

Marius had made his way to the door. "Don't worry about a thing, Sergeant. Your secret is safe with me," he laughed out loud and closed the door behind him.

Joe listened to the door click shut before beginning to finish undressing for bed. While brushing his teeth, Joe heard the door click open without a knock, and he heard his youngest soldier, Robert Parker, calling out for him.

"Bruthing muy teef, thude."

Parker appeared around the corner of the doorway to the bathroom, "Cigar Cubano, Sergeante?"

Joe spit out the foam and washed it down the drain. "Kid, that ain't Cuban grass, no matter how much you pretend it is."

"But it smells so good with its small touch of cherry and vanilla. I hope, a mellow burn afterward."

"Parker, you almost sound like a true cigar connoisseur."

"Do you wish to partake or not, Sergeant? I was thinking we could sit out on the balcony and throw rocks at the city until sun comes up; kinda see how many hajji we could hit in the head. Eh?"

"How in the hell can you have any energy after a thirty-six hour shift?"

"I have all this pent up sexual energy, so I burn it up by making dumb contests out of everything."

"Parker, do you really want me to tell you how I burn that energy up?"

"Sergeant Busch, it's actually very unhealthy for you to fire off as many knuckle children as you do. You'll be blind someday, and I'm gonna' laugh at you while I sit on the sunny beach in California."

"Parker, I'm going to give you to the count of five to get out of my room before I use my stripes to make life hell for you. Go find Marius. He's doing mail call. He'll smoke it with you. "

"This is a real fine Cuban..."

"Like I said, one...three..."

"You skipped a number."

"I outrank you. I don't have to count correctly. Four..."

"I'm gone."

Joe listened to the door shut slightly harder than a few minutes earlier and grinned to himself. He thought about the kid from California whom he'd just kicked out of his room. Parker was borderline husky with a boyish face still freckled with acne. Two fingers on his left hand, his pinky and ring, were permanently bent from a poor landing after a parachute training jump at jump school.

He knew that, too often, he looked out more than he should for Parker because he thought of the Golden State kid more as the little brother he never had rather than the soldier he was. He doubted that if the time came if he could ever order Parker into harm's way and would rather put his own life in danger in a heartbeat.

After writing a short letter to Sara, Joe turned in to fall asleep.

Chapter Two

Joe knew his dad had finished chores and was most likely sitting at the small kitchen table in the old farmhouse. His father, a lifelong farmer, had taken over the family farm early in his marriage and raised a family of eight, five daughters and three sons. He worked hard to teach his children the husbandry of the land and animals. Years of good yields and others of drought had begun to take their toll on the leathered face of the old farmer. Joe admired his father and looked up to him as his hero who had served during Vietnam. His father could still do anything, and would beat him soundly in a game of horse under the bent basketball rim in the loft of the barn.

Kelli, his youngest sister and last one of the children still in high school, would be up in her bedroom pretending to be working on homework while talking to her boyfriend. Sue, Joe's mother, would be finishing the dishes and looking forward to a nightly rerun of MASH. He hoped his mom might write a letter to him before calling it a night.

Joe remembered the day he joined the Army, not yet out of high school, and how Sue would not say a word to him for almost three weeks. They would even eat supper together, and she wouldn't acknowledge that he was there. This memory still made him chuckle to himself as he lay under the covers of his bed nine thousand miles away from his twin bed at home.

Joe rolled over and tucked the sheets between his knees and switched his thoughts to his "American pie sweetheart," Sara

Broshen. She was the gigantic secret that he wanted to scream to the world.

They started dating when they were in high school. Joe even remembered that he had been mowing hay the entire day before their first date and had a horrible sunburn the night he picked her up and met her parents. They had broken up when he shipped off to basic training, but he had managed to rekindle the flame on his leave before this tour, his second, in Iraq.

His thoughts shifted to their last night together when he had been on leave. He fluffed the pillow under his head hoping the cool side of the pillow would work its magic. He pictured Sara...she had been so beautiful that night.

While on furlough, Joe had heard that Sara would be home from college for her fall break the following weekend. He remembered his nervousness while he dialed her number later that night rivaled how he felt on their first date. She answered her phone, and he was speechless by the sound of her voice. He felt almost like a stalker as he took a breath but still couldn't talk until she said, "Hello?" again.

"Hey, ummm, it's Joe. You remember me?" was all he could muster.

"Oh, my God! Joe! It's been so long. How have you been?" Sara said with almost another dozen questions about him and his new life in the Army.

He couldn't recall much more of the conversation but remembered how he felt after he asked if she wanted to go out for a beer. "I'd love to see you again, Joe," Sara said.

He went over to her house two days later. While waiting for her, he talked with her folks and answered her family's, especially her little brother's, questions about the Army. Had he ever killed anyone? He reassured her younger sibling that he had never killed anyone but had seen a lot of scary places in Iraq. Sara and Joe left and went out to relive old times and meet old friends at the The English Pub, Dyersville's old, Irish watering hole. They sat in a far back corner.

Drink after drink went down smoothly, and the time flew by while they shared stories of bad relationships and mistakes they had made during their time apart. Joe listened to stories of nursing school, and Sara was astonished by the crazy things the guy sitting across from her had done. They made her accomplishments at school seem pretty timid.

They lost track of time until the lights came on in the bar and were all alone with the barkeep telling them it was time to go home. They walked out together and looked up at the October night sky. The car ride home to her place was quiet with late night radio playing 80's love songs. He drove with one hand because the other was being held by the softest hands he had ever felt.

When they got back to her house, Sara asked if he wanted to come back to the deck and look up at the stars the way they used to. Joe held onto her hip while she led the way through her parents' darkened house, around the dining room table and past the blanket chest. They walked out onto the deck where the dark blue and black sky was lighted up by millions of twinkling flecks of light floating down onto Sara's shoulder length hair, settling in her eyes.

Joe turned over and found it difficult to fall asleep after being awake for thirty-six hours at a time. When a body was awake for that long, falling asleep, even with soothing memories, turned into a chore. He rolled over to face the wall next to his bed and squirreled himself deeper under the sheets. He started to feel sleep creeping into his bones as his brightly lit room in Baghdad tried to wipe out the memory of his last night with his sweetheart, and he pulled the blankets over his head.

Securely tucked under the covers and on the deep precipice of sleep, he thought back to the last night he had been with Sara. He had shown Sara which stars to look for to find his favorite-the one on which he had wished he may and he wished he might have the wish he wished that night. He remembered what it had felt like when Sara lay by his side. He had traced with his finger the path from Orion's belt, forged eastward through the darkest of blues, to a glimmering red star that Joe always made his wishes.

"Do you think it's all right for us both to wish on the same star?" she asked.

"Sara, that's the wish that got me through my first deployment. I always hoped that you would be wishing the same wish on the same star."

"And what wish would that be?" Sara whispered lifting her head from his chest and gazing at him.

"You," Joe said softly and gently grasped her chin and deeply kissed her.

She pulled close until they felt as one.

The war still raged outside Room 701. Inside, a soldier found peace in a hell that would return to Joe's mind in ways only the devil could muster before he re-awakened to the city and its war.

Joe slipped into the murky, deep, and powerful depths of the unconscious that ruled his slumber. His tired and battle-battered mind hid itself in dreams of home and traveled across the deserts and oceans, mountains and rivers, and to a haunted place that had plagued his psyche since he had been ordered to return to this dirty city in the ancient lands of Mesopotamia.

He rolled and tossed under the sheets in the broken land of a horrible reality.

His world whirled around him when he replayed standing under his family's flagpole in a swirling fog with the flag he wore on his right shoulder, draped around him. Hot tears rolled down his cheeks while he watched his parents locked in a heart-rending embrace in front of his family's home. There were no sounds from the fertile fields and a silent wind blew through his mother's hair.

Two strangers stood at a short distance with their hands held humbly clasped behind their backs. One of the men wore all black without expression. The other wore a familiar green uniform with brass buttons on his lapels, ribbons stacked high on his chest, and a beret. He looked in Joe's direction, through Joe, and at the flag that hung limply in a silent breeze. No lips or nose were on that man's face, but his eyes showed his pained expression that war has a cost in blood that whole families must pay while he stared above a flag draped Joe at the wilted stars and stripes on the country family's flagstaff.

Joe's vision slowly floated over the hazy ground to another form, a new one he had not noticed before in the familiar and frequent dream. A figure started to materialize when it stepped from behind the thick trunk of the maple tree his father planted in the front yard when he married Joe's mother some 35 years ago. The unfamiliar figure failed to wholly materialize any more than showing that it bore the shape and curves of a young woman.

She advanced out of the shadow of the maple tree and carved a trench with one hand in the foggy ground. She closed the shallow furrow with a breath, and a sapling grew quick and fast while she caressed the budding leaves of the young tree. She kept her back to Joe whose streaming tears rolled down his cheeks, over the blue field of stars and red stripes before disappearing into the rising fog.

Joe's vision was torn away from the stunning seedling and back to his mom. She saw his tears falling fast and called out to him with the love of a mother. The silent world of his dream yearned to be shattered by her voice. But the thick veil of rising mist would not be torn, and it swallowed his home and parents with a sharp crack of light.

Joe felt himself begin to fall once the ground tore open under his feet. He soared downward still wrapped in the flag as he felt his whole world being ripped away. The colors flipped and flapped until they completely engulfed him. The hissing of the fog grew louder, stronger until he screamed and felt himself crash into another plane of consciousness.

"Busch. Man. Wake the hell up!"

Joe snapped back to reality with light blazing around him and a suffocating blanket wrapped around him. He struck out and grabbed onto whoever was shaking and suffocating him. His adrenal glands flooded his blood with inhuman strength and returned the favor of suffocation as he kicked himself free from the strangling bedspread.

"Aghgh...let...go...of...me."

The voice was unexpectedly familiar, and Joe realized where he was and that he was choking his best friend and roommate, SGT Greg Forrester. Joe released his choke hold and clambered backward on the bed until he felt the headboard against his back. "Greg?"

Greg felt at his throat and tried to catch his breath.

Joe shook his head. "Man, I'm sorry. You woke me up in the middle of a dream. I had no clue what I was doing."

Greg coughed again. "I know. I know. You were freaking me out. I had to wake you up. I just didn't think you would try to kill me in the process."

"I'm sorry..." Joe whispered hoarsely.

"It's okay. It's okay." Greg had caught his breath and had gotten to his feet, still rubbing his neck.

"What time is it?"

"It's eleven. You don't have to be anywhere important for another hour."

Joe laid his head back against the wall with the top of the headboard at the base of his neck and took a deep breath. "Somehow I doubt that I'll be able to close my eyes for another twenty minutes..."

"Yeah, dude. After that, I'm never waking you up again. Besides, if you fall asleep, I'm going to sneak over there and choke you. I owe you one now."

Joe said chuckling, "Yeah, I guess you do." Another deep breath and he hid his shaking right hand under the bed spread covering his legs.

He slowly got up and stretched. Another day in hell.

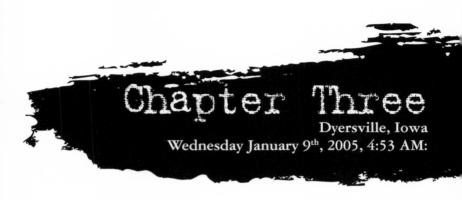

Chapter Three

Dyersville, Iowa
Wednesday January 9th, 2005, 4:53 AM:

A queasy Sara Broshen cracked open her eyelids and looked at the blinking red eyes on her nightstand. The clock stared back at her in the early morning, gray light. Four fifty-three did not register in her sleepy mind. Her stomach tied itself in another knot forcing her out of bed. It was almost too painful to walk to the bathroom just down the hall.

What had she eaten last night? The question gnawed at her. Hunched over, Sara walked through the dark hallway dimly lit by a nightlight. The wooden floorboards creaked softly when she shuffled down the runner in the corridor. One hand attempted to quell her tangled insides, the other sliding along the wall on her right steadying her shaky legs.

She crept into the bathroom and shut the door as quietly as possible. Tommy, her six year old brother, who slept in the room next to the bathroom, was known to wake up at the click of the door being shut in the middle of the night. Sara's tummy growled and groaned while entwining itself in another impossibly crushing cramp forcing a sour and bitter acidic taste up the back of her tongue.

The achingly cold seat shocked the blood out of her legs when she sat down. "Why do I even bother to shave?" she asked when the flow began, and she felt some of the pressure relieved before being driven over to the wall in a crunched-up ball of unbearable pain. What was the matter with her? She had never been this sick in her entire life. What had she done to deserve this? Sara rested her forehead on the roll of Charmin stuck halfway out the wall.

The roll of dissolvable wipes absorbed her tears as she moaned from the pain between her hips. Just a roll of toilet paper, a cardboard tube wrapped in double ply, quilted softness against her forehead snapped her spirit in two. Sara broke down and wept because in her Joe's last letter to her from the war, he complained that the toilet paper in the hotel he was living in and fighting from would chafe his behind. He requested, in the letter, some monkey butt powder if she got the chance to put some in her next package to him.

She swallowed a sob and flattened the topside of the roll with her elbow. She wiped her eyes clear. Sara finished her morning routine on the toilet, and she challenged herself to suck up the pain like she knew Joe always did. He wouldn't let himself be kept down with an upset stomach. Endeavoring to swallow the pain and salty tears, she got up to wash her hands.

Sara bent over and made her way to the sink and leaned against it. The bright, white light glinting off the polished chrome handles forced her eyes shut. She felt her stomach forcing its way into her throat. Tumbling backward, she landed on her backside and twisted around to clutch the porcelain bowl. The few remaining bits of last night's supper rode on a geyser of stomach acid through her esophagus and erupted from her mouth and nose. The taste burned her sinuses and dripped off the tip of her nose before she could find the handle to flush the disgusting gray mess into the septic tank.

A small wave of relief washed over the beaches of her mind before the tsunami of another caustic eruption of stomach fluids began. Bout after bout of dry heaves followed, wrenching the knots tighter. Veins in Sara's forehead seemed about to burst from the pressure of the horrendous vomiting. Her stomach

fought to reach into her small intestine and pull something...
anything up with the anguishing spasms of her belly.

What was wrong with her? It couldn't be what she had
eaten. She hadn't eaten anything out of the ordinary. Not food
poisoning. Everyone else would be sick, too. It wasn't that
time of the month...was it? Sara moaned.

She sprinted through her mental notes about her monthly
cycle. She'd had one last month. The month before? Sara
could feel her breasts through Joe's tee shirt, which she wore to
bed every night. They felt almost normal, a little swollen, but
that was normal for her since her next cycle was supposed to
start the following week. Wait...they had been kind of tender a
few days before, but wasn't that because she had been running
lately to try and shed the few pounds she'd put on since Joe
left? Her previous periods were normal, light at first, a day or
two of heavy and then a quick taper to the finish.

"No. No, it can't be!"

She moaned quietly. The mental sprint Sara ran through
her memory tripped on the last hurdle she tried to jump.

It was only once. She was on the pill. She hadn't missed a
pill in months. Not even the placebo ones. Never.

The tears fell hard and fast, streaking down her flushed
cheeks. The morning sickness forgotten. Tommy, the light
sleeper next door, forgotten. She crawled over to the feminine
supplies under the sink praying that her mom didn't have any.

The blue tampon box. The pink pad box. A bottle of
Midol. They were tucked away in the back corner past the trap
in the drain. "Please, God, no, I can't, not now...." she prayed,
wiping her eyes.

Sara pulled out one of the wrappers still sealed as tightly as
the day it left the factory. It felt like a pen wrapped in a thin
wax paper. Sara tightly gripped it and backed out from under
the sink and let the cabinet doors slam shut. With one arm on

the countertop, she pulled herself up and looked at the wreck in the mirror. Her brown hair was frazzled, her eyes puffy from crying, and her cheeks streaked and red when the tri-fold mirrors revealed their secret.

The little, brown canister stared back at her with her name typed on the sticker. The yellow warning sticker stared at her. It tore her life and dreams apart with the printed words on it. The warning was as plain and simple as the words the pharmacist said, which replayed in her mind. Her reply to the woman behind the prescription pick-up counter at the drugstore rang endlessly as her tired mind picked itself up and crawled to the bitter truth.

The scene ran on a never ending loop in her mind with the main character in a starring role. Miss Sara Broshen, under the lights of the drug store highlighting all her features, and her emphatically responding to the mature pharmacist, "I don't have to worry about a thing. I won't be doing any of that anytime soon."

"Honey, if it was as simple as that, there would be a lot fewer of us running around here," the pharmacist told her. "I have to tell you that this antibiotic will make the pill ineffective."

Forty-eight hours later, with her sinus infection clearing up, Joe called to see if she wanted to catch up on life.

Chapter Four

Dyersville, Iowa
Wednesday January 9th, 2005, 5:30 AM,
9 hours behind Baghdad:

The day's beginning sunlight filtered through the oak tree that shaded the Broshen family house. Inside, Sara sat dazed. Her hands lay in her lap with the pregnancy test sitting on the countertop just in front of her.

"What do I do?" she whispered weakly. What can I do? What choice do I have if this turns blue? Sara thought about the improbability, the impossibility of a negative result. How would she tell him? How would she tell her family? How do I tell his family?

Sara glanced up with a torn look in her eyes. She desperately hoped for not a single change in color, not even a single shade or trace of blue. Her career, her dreams of getting out of this small town in the middle of a giant American cornfield hung on the outcome. She prayed for a miracle. Her heart skipped a beat at the thought of Joe's child growing inside her womb. Sara's hand unconsciously reached out and brought the stick within inches of her face so she could watch the transition finish.

The blue line seemed to flash like a bolt from a cross bow. It carried with it a message full of questions as the early morning battle wound down in Sara's mind. The pregnancy test clattered to the ceramic tile floor, and a scared whisper escaped her lips to the reflection in the mirror. "I have to tell Joe."

Sara struggled back to bed and tried to shut out the painful morning sickness, burying herself under the covers of her bed. She wrapped the sheets around her as tightly as she could and pulled them even tighter around her body, hiding her head under a pillow. The enormity of her condition sprouted like the first springtime bud of a crocus that had lain dormant through the cold months of the winter. The flower pushed through the frosty soil, ready to spring open to show the world how beautiful the first flower of spring can be.

Worries. Fears. Joys. Promises of a lifetime full of trials and challenges to be celebrated by milestones like her mother's. Everything discovered before her loomed up from deep inside Sara. She released the suffocating cocoon she wrapped herself in and rolled over to stare out the window. The winter sun peeked over the horizon and reflected the secrets of the early morning light off the fresh powdery snow. Yesterday's footpaths through the snow had been wiped out by the new covering.

Sara fluffed the pillow she covered herself with and propped herself back against it. Why couldn't she obliterate the pregnancy test like the snow had covered everything outdoors? She pulled Joe's tee shirt off to gaze at her flat belly.

She ran her hands over her abdomen and began to plan how to tell her family and Joe's family. Echoes of the early morning fight still rang under the pounding heart inside her chest. She let the winter sunshine fill her world with hope.

"We'll get through this together," she whispered. "We will let your daddy know all about you, and he will be home as soon as he can. I promise, Baby, I promise. I promise."

Tears of joy rolled down her cheeks. One streaked off her chin and caught a beam of sunlight as it fell to her breast just over her heart. Sara hugged herself and continued cooing to her and Joe's new wonder of life.

Chapter Five

Baghdad, Iraq.
Wednesday, January 9th, 2005, 1130 hours,
9 hours ahead of Dyersville, Iowa:

"Gentlemen! Form up!" Sergeant Joseph Busch barked at his fire team while he stowed a fresh pack of smokes.

Joe assembled his team in the upstairs ballroom of the Sheraton Hotel for the preconvoy briefing. The Command Quarters shared a common wall in the next room and squawky voices from the radios that scanned his unit's, and battalion's, frequencies.

The six men in front of him stood almost shoulder to shoulder in a straight line that was divided into two separate groups. Sergeant Reed, a black man from South Carolina, was on the left. The line of troops continued with the medic, SPC Jones, or Doc, followed by PFC Juan Zapatto, the squad's token Rican. PFC Robert Taylor finished up the first group with his arms folded in front of him resting on the ammo pouches hanging on the front of his body armor. He let his weapon dangle from the D-ring that clipped that sling to his vest.

The second group was headed up by SPC Alan Finn, another Iowan who looked as if he was raised strictly on meat and potatoes. With his strong build, blond hair, and blue eyes, Finn was a giant of a man who would fit in perfectly with Nazi Germany. SPC Sean Parker stood next to Finn. He smelled the left over stub of his unfinished Cuban cigar from the earlier that morning. His pudgy face and shorter height made him the butt of too many jokes that he countered as effectively as a late night comedy show host.

"SGT Reed, is the squad ready to roll out?"

"Roger, SGT Busch. PCI's and PCC's are complete."

"Good, listen up, fella's. This is just a mail run over to battalion. Quick and easy over the river. You know the rules of engagement, but I don't think that we're going to see anything too exciting since hajji doesn't like to engage in the middle of the day. Remember to steer clear of trash in the road. They can still fire off an IED from inside a coffee shop and walk away like nothing happened."

"SGT Busch, are we taking our usual spots in the trucks?"

"Yeah, Zappy, you'll be driving SGT Reed with Taylor manning his SAW in the turret. Parker, you're my driver as usual, and I'll lead the convoy with Finn gunning the .50 cal. Doc, you can ride in either of the trucks, I don't care which one you're in as long as you're not trying to pick off dogs with your nine mill'. We're going back out at last light to cruise the strip. You can have your fun then. Got it?"

"Roger, Sergeant." Doc pretended to act hurt that he couldn't get another "kill."

"Any other questions?" Joe waited a second before continuing. "Then start heading downstairs and fire up the trucks. Fall out!"

The squad made its way to the elevator, and Joe found himself in his unit's office to update his squad's status on the whiteboard.

He made the necessary marks on the board and stopped to look at the map of Baghdad next to the status board. Yellow-headed pins marked any action that had occurred in the city limits over the last 12 hours. Red pins marked where any unit had taken casualties, and a cluster of yellow pins surrounded two red pins in the northwestern sector.

Joe gathered his thoughts and didn't acknowledge the private who stood watch over the radios before walking out to the elevator that was just returning to the top floor. The brass doors dinged open and he pushed the ground floor button as he leaned against the side of the box that hung on cables 200 feet in the air. He conducted his own precombat inventory and precombat checks of himself by making sure that he had his necessary rounds and chambered one in his weapon that hung at his side.

A ten second ride and a short walk led him downstairs and out of the hotel into the brisk January of the desert. He walked to the trucks that his men had brought around to the entrance before taking a long look at the city surrounding him. Neighboring buildings scraped at the sky and trash piled in the gutters of the street. Diesel exhaust fumes filled his nose, and a six-and-a-half-pound weapon hung at his side. His eyes searched for open windows where danger easily hid.

Joe opened the door to the armored HMMWV and settled in.

"Ready, Sergeant?" Parker asked as he dropped the truck into drive.

Busch grabbed the handset to the radio and keyed it, "Cobra Seven One, this is Cobra One One over."

"One One, this is Seven One. Go ahead."

"Roger Seven One, be advised I am leaving the hotel with two victors and seven personnel on the mail run to battalion, time now. How copy over?"

"One One, I copy you leaving the hotel with two victors and seven packs. Time now. Over?"

"That's a good copy Seven One, One One out." Joe signed off the radio conversation.

"Let's roll out, Parker." He ordered the convoy to take off to the sound of Finn chambering a round home in the fifty caliber machine gun in the turret just behind his left shoulder.

Chapter Six

Joe finished filling out the after action review paperwork required after every patrol, mail run, or shopping spree. He walked back to where his soldiers were waiting in the mezzanine of the hotel they called home. His silent and trained steps in tan canvas boots took him to the elevator. After calling the elevator to the top floor, he reached into his cargo pocket on the outside of his right leg just above his knee. After feeling around the extra magazine loaded with thirty rounds, he found the familiar rectangular box with a matchbook tucked between the plastic covering and the cardboard. His helmet hung off the front of his body armor by the fastened chinstrap routed over one of three magazine holders fastened to the outside of the Kevlar lined with a ceramic plate. He pulled out of the pocket, flipping open the top of the red and white box and raised it to his lips. He removed a butt from the half empty pack of cigarettes when the elevator dinged its arrival behind two brass doors.

Trained and disciplined, Joe flexed his calloused hand around the weapon and prepared to defend himself against the possible and unknown danger that might lie in the confines of the elevator. With an unlit cigarette dangling between his lips he stepped to the side as the doors began to part. Seeing that he was still alone, he stepped into the brass box with a giant window that overlooked the city.

Twinkling lights of yellows and fluorescent whites floated on unseen breezes and filled the elevator window overlooking the city. Two Apache helicopters armed with missiles and machine guns fluttered over the northwestern district. Joe could see the next patrol from his unit leaving the hotel's entrance nineteen stories below him. He observed every member of the ten-man team assume their individual offensive postures of patrolling.

The brass doors clanged shut behind him, and he turned away from the dazzling picture of Baghdad and pressed the button for seventh floor where his team waited for the word. His reflection in the polished luxury brass stared the Sergeant in the eyes and looked deeply into his soul. The reflection was looking at a man in the middle of another 36 hour shift and grown more than a patchy 5 o'clock shadow. His soul bared an empty stomach that was too tired to find food and lungs that ached for the cigarette in his lips to be lit.

The lines around the eyes told a story of sleeping only four hours every other day and the nightmares of the probability that one of his men might be killed on the streets. Canvas boots on their second deployment had walked more miles than Joe could remember, but he remembered every improvised explosive device that he had walked or driven past. In permanent marker, a simple A POS was written to set apart the wearer's blood type. Under the Sergeant's right arm hid the meat tag tattoo that would forever scar and identify him.

The elevator bumped to a stop, and the bell rang.

Yanked from searching into his soul, the doors opened onto a scene from a Hollywood movie. Juan and Rob were crashed against the hallway wall with their body armor hanging open and weapons propped over their legs, magazines still locked in. The squad's machine gunner's M249 SAW lay on its bipod legs with a belt of 100 rounds draped over the barrel by the door that led to the patio. Finn and Parker stood there smoking while staring at the stars and streaks of tracers that erupted throughout the city.

Joe stepped through the patio doors and faced the tired men who trusted their lives to his decisions. His men knew each other well enough that they could read one another like a book. Words did not have to be spoken to know their day was finally over. Juan nudged a sleeping Rob while Parker and Finn took another drag before flicking their smokes over the edge to fall seventy feet.

Taking his hand off the slung weapon on his side for the first time in hours, Joe motioned everyone to gather on the patio for the briefing. "Everyone on the patio. Let's go, you lazy bastards."

Rob's knees popped as he rose and stretched. Juan reached out and grabbed his battle buddy's hand for assistance in getting off the floor, and the pair walked through the door to the crisp, dirty air of Baghdad. Parker and Finn snagged the two seats outside. Juan leaned on one arm over the rail, and Rob knelt on the worn out pad that covered his knee. Everyone, minus the machine gunner, Finn, covered the trigger holes on their individual weapons and rested their thumbs on the selector levers. Eight sets of eyes surveyed the rooftops for any danger to the squad while their Joe lifted the cover on his book of matches and ripped out a cardboard stick. He closed the cover and held the book in his left hand and struck the match with his right. The tiny light shimmered and grew as he raised it to the end of the cheap cigarettes. The match lit the tobacco and after a deep drag filled the man's lungs with heat and fire that fed the ache in his chest. He flicked his wrist to put out the match and tossed it into the ashtray. Light gray smoke trailed from his nose.

"Gentleman, I am friggin' tired and need some sleep, so I won't keep you long. We are going back out in 6 hours at

0400. I'll let the guard shift know to wake everyone up 0300 so we can prep the vehicles. It is a mounted patrol, and we will be on the streets killing hajji bastards until sometime around noon. Finn, you can leave your personal weapon at the desk upstairs. You'll be manning the .50 cal. Be sure to draw the ammo on time. Everyone else, you know the deal, so wake up, shit, shave, and get your asses in gear to give the trucks a look-over before we head out."

Joe took another drag and looked around at Rob who was in high school at this time last year chasing cheerleaders and skipping classes.

"You okay, Rob? You look like something's bothering you."

"Yeah, Sergeant. I just got a dear john from home. I think I need a smoke. You got one?"

"We got another one to start fellas...it's all downhill after Mr. All American football player takes a drag from an Iraqi smoke. You sure about this?"

The team chuckled and cheered him on to an early death.

"You ain't got the balls to light it up!" Parker heckled.

"Let's hear the cough. C'mon, let's hear it," Finn said adding his two cents worth.

"Lemme see someone's lighter."

Parker and Finn raced to get their Zippos out of their pockets. Joe beat everyone to it by tossing his book to the new smoker. "Think you can handle this, kid?" he chided.

"Shut the fuck up, Sarge!"

It took Rob two strikes to get the match lit and take his first drag. The smoke filled his mouth and stung its way down his windpipe to his clean lungs. The cherry on the end of the smoke lit up the lines around his eyes and the day's growth of beard. His body rejected the smoke with a cough that would make a doctor cringe. Cheers rang out from the team around him as Rob brought the smoke back to his lips and hit the nail a little farther into his coffin. This drag brought the nicotine to his brain and fingertips. He felt the tingling sensation deep in his toes and his tired muscles in his thighs. He exhaled through his nose and smelled the smoke penetrate his sinuses. The city and hotel patio began to spin when he reached out to hold onto his best friend's shoulder to make it stop spinning.

"This is so awesome making another smoker out of Mr. Goody-two-shoes," Finn said. "Someone remind me when I write to his girl later to thank her and that I'm looking forward to seeing her when I get back."

"Up yours, man."

"Hey, dude, she's free now, and if she wants some good, city boy loving, I will be more than happy to do what you couldn't."

"Now we just gotta' get him in the titty bars when we get home," Parker added. "I know a girl that wouldn't mind taking that pesky, little virginity chip off his shoulders. She'll show you things that you didn't know a woman could do, Rob."

"I still can't believe that you deployed without getting laid, man," Joe said. "Don't you know that the virgin always dies first?"

"I am going to kick your ass when the spinning stops, Sergeant. You're not supposed to say shit like that."

Joe smiled. "It is funny, though, isn't it, boys?"

Everyone on the team chuckled and added more comments to the new smoker before Joe took another drag and finished his brief. "Anyways, gentlemen, we need to get going and get some sleep. It's going to be a long day tomorrow. Now get the hell out of my sight. I'm tired of smelling your sweaty asses. Rob, stick around for a minute."

The team rose and headed into the hotel and their rooms to shower and rack out for a few hours. Weapons and Kevlar body armor swung back and forth while they made their way through the doors when Finn laughed aloud to Parker, "Isn't it cute that the Sarge and Rob are having a little romantic date on the patio?"

Parker turned back to the open doors to the patio. "Hey, Sergeant, just because his girl broke up with him doesn't mean he's going to cuddle with you tonight."

Joe grinned and said, "You're the only one I want to sleep with, Parker."

The door swung shut behind the team, and the two men were alone on the patio. Joe finished his smoke and flicked it into the night. Rob sat down in one of the chairs and laid his head back with eyes shut.

"Still spinning?

"Yep."

"Don't worry, man. You'll get used to it, and it won't last long. So what did this chick say why she was breaking up with you?"

"Same reason every other chick breaks up with us when we deploy. She found another guy."

"Jody's a prick, isn't he?" Joe said alluding to the man named Jody who stole girlfriends when their men were gone.

"He's a son of a bitch."

"Don't let it keep you down for long. If she couldn't wait for someone who is almost dying so she can live in America, she isn't good enough for you."

"I know, I know."

"You sure you're OK? Anything else you want to talk about, man?"

"Nah, I think I'm good."

"Well, you should sleep well with a little nicotine in your system. I'll see you in the morning, man."

"Goodnight, Sergeant, thanks for the talk."

"Anytime you need anything, you know I'll always be here. Hajji's a bastard, and we gotta' stick together to get the rest of us home."

"Shoot first, and ask questions later."

"Goodnight."

He laid a hand on the private's shoulder as he walked by him and into the hotel. He turned left and opened his armored vest while walking to Room 701 at the end of the hall. The third door on his right was open, and he glimpsed into PFC Johannes's room as he walked past.

Doug sat next to a cheap end table watching an Iraqi news show broadcast in Arabic on the room's television and smoking a cigarette while cleaning his M4. The weapon lay on the table opened up like a shotgun with its guts spread out. The PFC held the bolt as he brushed the carbon residue off the face of the bolt. A cigarette dangled from his lips while he inspected the parts one by one using the glow from the Arabic news show.

Joe pulled his room key from his breast pocket, and his fingers brushed against the angel medallion that he received for Christmas from his Sara back home in Iowa. The dime-sized, precious medal was etched with the word "strength" on the back. An angel with a sword stood out on the front. He kept it next to his heart where he stored memories of Sara. As he unlocked the door to the room on the eastern corner of the hotel, he recalled their first date three years before. He smirked when he remembered meeting her parents for the first time and how her dad had tried to be Mr. Tough guy before he let his daughter out on their first date.

He walked into the room and saw his best friend tucked under the sleeping bag on a bed in the corner. Sergeant Greg Forrester shot up like a bolt and grabbed his weapon instinctively raising it.

"I swear to God if you shoot me, I will beat you to death with that weapon, motherfucker. Damn, it's just me, man. Relax!"

"Knock next time, damnit!"

"Dude, seriously why would hajji try to sneak in through the door when he could come in the window from the balcony above ours?"

"I'm still half asleep. Don't make me think. I have to get up in a few hours."

"Cry me a river. I have to get up at oh-three to get the guys up."

"How was the tour today?"

"The usual, went up to New York, circled around to Pennsylvania, and ended up on Boardwalk. Nothing special. Still cross-eyed from looking through those damn night vision goggles."

"I hear ya', Bro." Greg was awake now. "I grabbed your mail, and it's on your bed. Another letter from Sara is there. Smells nice, too."

"Did you read it, too?"

"Why would I want to read your sex letter when I have my own girl who writes to me?"

"Mail sex, huh? Guess if I were a two-minute man like you, I would need to do it in the mail just to last as long as a regular guy."

"That's too funny, man. Hey, watch out in the shower. A few of my knuckle children are probably still on the wall." Greg tried to gross his best friend out.

"At least our kids can play together then."

Greg chuckled. "That's nasty, man,"

"Hey, I got a question for you before you go back to sleep."

"Make it quick. I'm tired yet."

"I am thinking about asking Sara to marry me, but I don't have a ring. Think it would be okay to send my class ring instead?"

Greg lay back down and pulled the covers up to his shoulders, fluffed his pillow, and closed his eyes. "Sounds like a great idea. Go for it. I know she'll probably say no because I already asked her to marry me."

"Thanks for the vote of confidence. Go to sleep. Your ugly ass needs some beauty sleep."

"Goodnight, sweetheart."

"That's gay, man."

"Want to cuddle tonight?"

"No, I don't want to cuddle. I have my own bed and a letter that smells like home. Stop with the gay talk, or I might take you up on the offer. It's been a while since I held someone."

"I was joking. But, I think you're serious about that though."

"Keep talking shit. See what happens."

"I love you, cupcake."

"I love you, too, sweetheart." Joe played the game just to get his buddy to shut up.

"Such a homo," Greg said as he slipped back into sleep.

Joe had dropped his Kevlar vest and helmet at the foot of his own bed and sat down to unlace his boots. He reached over to flip through his mail and saw a letter from his dad, one from his sister, and the tell-tale faded green envelope that held Sara's letter. He reached down and pulled the knife off his body armor and slipped it behind the seal on the envelope. One small tug and a pull, and the blade cleanly opened the letter. He immediately recognized the scent of Victoria's Secret called "Lucky" that wafted to his nose.

The letter was written on blue stationary with a border filled with stars. The blue faded from a dark night into a dusk blue in the center criss-crossed with crease lines. Sara's handwriting flowed over the front and spilled onto the back in a swooping cursive that mixed with printing. He laid the note on the bed next to him before he bent over to untie the bloused pants and unlace his boots. The laces fell open, and he kicked his boots off when he picked the note up and began to read...

Dear Joe,   *December 17th, 2004*

Hey, babe, how are you doing over there? Staying safe I pray. I cannot sleep tonight, again. I was at Mom and Dad's this afternoon, and Dad had the news on. I tried not to pay attention to it, but I could not help but hear that more guys our age are dying every day in that city. I pray every day that you will come home to me again. I have been a nervous wreck lately. I miss you so much, and I hope that you do not think I am writing too much to you. Your friends there must think I am crazy. It seems like I can't write enough to you, though. There is a void in my life, and when I write to you, I feel like I am actually talking to you. Do you remember how we used to talk on the phone until midnight or later at night? I really miss those long talks. I know I have told this before, but I feel like I can tell you anything and you will not think I am weird. I loved hearing you tell me Army stories even though I had no idea what you were talking about. Did you know that it was two months ago last week, probably three by the time you get this, that we saw each other last? How did I make it this long without seeing you? I love when you call me late at night. I know you do not get to a phone very often, but next time you do, I'll be waiting to hear your sweet voice again. I am sorry I wasn't able to answer my phone when you called last Sunday. I was in church, and everyone looked at me really crazy when my phone started to ring. I could have sworn it was on silent. I guess I should probably change the ringer from "You shook me all night long" to something a little bit more appropriate if I am going to have to put up with a phone ringing in church. I am pretty sure my reputation with the old ladies is ruined after they heard that. When Dad found out that it was your ring, he said he will have to have a little chit-chat with you when you get back. Something about shooting you on sight or something, but by then, being shot at won't be something new to you. Just kidding, Babe. I know he looks up to you like my little brothers do. But I should probably get going and wrap this up before I start crying again. Joe, I miss you so very much that it hurts my heart to think what I would do without you in my life. I hope you don't think this is too forward, but I hope to have you in my life for a long time to come. We have to talk about that when you get home in December after this deployment is over. I know you read my letters to find those three little words, but you will have to wait a few more lines, Babe. Thanks for being there to read my letters. I feel a lot better now. You are 8,000 miles away, and you can still give me butterflies and make my lips miss your sweet kiss. I want you to know you are my whole world, and, Honey....I LOVE YOU SO MUCH. Take care of yourself, Babe, and bring yourself home to me soon. I love you.

I will love you always,
Sara

Joe kissed the letter and felt tears form. He looked through the window. "I love you, Sara."

Chapter Seven

Baghdad, Iraq.
Wednesday, January 9th, 2005, 2230 hours,
9 hours ahead of Dyersville, Iowa:

Joe reclined on his back and held the letter to his face as he breathed in his girlfriend's perfume. His arms fell to his lanky frame, and he began composing in his head the letter that he planned to write tonight asking Sara to be his wife. The letter fell from between his fingers while Joe began to unbutton his desert camouflage top. Four buttons later, the top was opened, and the belt loosened when Joe raised his tired body from the bed. He reached down and picked up his towel, stood, and turned to go into the bathroom.

Joe closed the door to the tiny room with a white porcelain toilet, bidet, and tub with a shower in it. The wall to the right held a giant mirror cracked in half from a past percussion from an explosion in the city. Paint flecked off the walls above the tiles that covered the wall to his chest height. A solitary light bulb lent a soft glow to the room as the Sergeant reached behind the curtain and turned on the water in the shower.

He stood in the center of the latrine and continued to strip, letting his pants fall in a heap on the floor around his ankles. Stepping out of the molehill of tan pants, he pulled the brown t-shirt over his head and let it fall on top of his pants. His green socks that stretched up over his calves were matted flat on the bottom from wearing and sweating in them for almost thirty-seven hours. The muscles in his legs barely contained the strength to stand straight while Joe checked out his physique in the mirror. His knobby knees were capped by a large knee cap, and his hips poked at the skin in the front of him.

The young man's six-pack strained through a light covering of belly fat while his chest resembled that of a farmer that threw hay in a barn all summer. His shoulders filled out over the deployment from supporting the fifty plus pounds of Kevlar, bulletproof plates on the front and back, and a battle load of 210 rounds. His right shoulder looked more developed than the left side. Joe surmised to himself that it grew that way from the extra weight of his weapon dangling from his right shoulder.

He reached up with a hand to feel the bump of a rib that never went back into place after being bucked by a heifer half the world away and years ago in his peaceful, prior life of living on his family's farm. His lower ribs showed their prominence through a thin layer of skin.

His neck was a whole shade darker than the rest of his white skin, some of it from a tan, mostly from sweat and dirt from the city where he fought all day and most of the nights. A thin five o'clock shadow was becoming foggy in the mirror from the steam filling the room. The lines and bags under the young man's brown eyes looked strong.

A swipe from his right hand streaked the mirror over his face and he leaned over the sink breathing in the steam. He rested on his left arm and stared into the dirty swipe on the mirror and wondered how and if he would ever get to see the land he grew up in and loved.

He looked into his own soul through his eyes to try and catch whatever attracted Sara to his heart. He wanted to see what so captured his young love's heart. Tired eyes began to cloud over and hide his own soul and asked even deeper questions of the young leader. Would he be able to get his men through another day? Would he be able to write the letter asking the woman he loved to be his wife? Would he ever breathe American air again? Joe looked deep into the eyes on the mirror, and he saw only shallow sockets where youth had lived only a year before.

He turned and slid the curtain open, reached up to turn the shower head to the side, and stepped into the tub sliding the thin plastic and wire loops on a rusty rod shut behind him. Timidly stepping into the hot water, he turned the shower head back onto him and turned around to let the water scald his back as he tried to cleanse himself from sins that constantly plagued his mind but never happened. He wanted nothing more than to make sure his men came home to their families in one piece.

This being his second deployment, it should have been easy. He wasn't as green as his men. Still his mind was plunged under doubts of his own leadership abilities. Stinging needles of water dug the sweat and dirt from his skin turning it tomato pink. He turned around and dipped his head under the torrent of purging water. Breathing out, he let the water scour some of the lines and bags from around the shallow sockets of his eyes.

He turned his mind from thoughts of his own inadequacy to that of his Sara back home. He wanted to tell her everything about his heart. He planned to tell her of the skipping rhythm that happened when he read her "I love you's." He wanted to share his dreams and aspirations of a place in the country where he knew they could live together and raise a family. He wanted to tell her all his secrets and present her with the keys to his heart, which she held in the tender palms of her sweet hands. Joe wanted to pull her close under the cleansing water of the Baghdad shower and lift her chin with his finger to kiss her beneath the water from the Euphrates. He wanted to feel her peering into his soul and know that she understood everything he didn't say. He wanted the world to give to her so that they could share in the greatest treasure that the blue pearl can give to two people. He simply wanted to look into her eyes and whispered to himself in the shower, "I love you, Babe. I'll be home before you know it."

The water began to cool down, and Busch finished up the shower in a hurry before he shut the water off. A silent drip plinked to the floor by his feet as he pulled his towel in and began to drying his arms and legs. He smelled the cheap shampoo he used to wash his clothes instead of detergent when he tussled his short hair in the brown towel. The curtain slid back, and he stepped out by the sink to look once more into his own eyes for the strength he would need to write the letter. He gazed into his steam-obscured reflection only for a moment before cinching the towel around his waist. Walking out through the door, he shut the light off in the bathroom to keep from waking his best friend sleeping across the room.

Joe stooped by the edge of his bed to reach under the mattress where he kept the paper and pen that he would write his letter on. Finding the supplies in their usual spot, he sat down on the bed and turned on his flashlight. He leaned it against the wall next to him lighting a haunting triangle and part of a circle on the ceiling. He slowly began to pour his heart out through his pen.

The Sergeant, who men around him looked up to and admired for being tough and disciplined, allowed his emotions to truly come out for the first time. He searched through the night for the words to tell his love about the feelings he held for her. His words flowed through hen-pecked handwriting, breaking only to stop and think of the next sentence that would bare his soul. His watch beeped the passing of the late hour, and he chose to wrap the letter up and ask the question on his mind and heart.

He pulled a small box from his stash of care packages from friends, family, and strangers showing their support for a soldier. He pulled the old mailing label off and wrote Sara's address on the box in its place. The return address simply stated that it was mailed from "Your Sergeant." The class ring on his pinky finger pulled off easily, and he opened up the pocket on the side of his duffel bag where he kept a second pair of dog tags. Joe opened the clasp on the long chain and slipped the beady metal chain through the ring and let it tumble down to the tag that caught the ring. He held the ring and chain in front of his face and kissed the ring before he placed it softly into the bottom of the box.

Joe folded the letter into thirds and then once more in half before stopping to write "I love you, Sara. See you soon." He put the letter into the box on top of his tags and ring, closed the cube, and set it on the floor by his weapon.

SGT Busch scooted down to the end of his bed and picked up his weapon from the floor where he left it before his shower. He pulled his weapon cleaning kit from between the mattress and box spring underneath him and wiggled with his weapon in one hand and his kit in the other to the lit end of the bed. Still clad only in a brown towel around his waist, he quickly disassembled his M4 Carbine.

Joe spread his weapon's parts in his lap. He brushed the carbon deposits off the face of the bolt, swabbed the barrel, and dusted the dirt from action slides. Ignoring the light from the flashlight, Joe reassembled his weapon in the dark and performed a functions check, making sure that the rifle would not misfire. He clapped the magazine back into its well and wiped the weapon with an old, oily t-shirt.

Joe leaned the weapon against the wall next to where he slept and turned the flashlight off. Darkness flooded the room, and the sounds of the city at night screamed in his ears as he pulled the covers back and climbed under them for a short four hours of sleep. Joe rolled over to face the wall and thought about the single thought and place for which every soldier pined. Home. He thought back to the pleasant days of cutting hay and daydreams where the buzz of mosquitoes turned into the whine of bullets whizzing past.

The thought about cutting hay before his first date with Sara brought forth a torrent of memories from their relationship and short time together. They had gone out for supper at a Perkin's Restaurant in Dubuque before making their way over to the theatre to buy tickets for a movie that he couldn't remember. He did remember how nervous he was during the drive into the city that night and how he fumbled even the most basic attempts at conversation the whole night long. He recalled stumbling and stuttering like a nervous schoolboy explaining to a teacher why he pulled some girl's hair at recess. His palms grew sweaty when he thought about how nervously he extended his hand during the movie to hold her hand. His heart skipped a beat when he felt the shock of Sara actually pulling his hand closer after intertwining their fingers.

He thought about how she never let go of his hand for the rest of the evening, even during another feeble attempt at making small talk on their drive back to Dyersville. The windows in the old Buick were rolled down on the drive home. Joe recalled how he had felt that July night with the wind blowing against his cheek, and the image of Sara's long, brown hair swirled in the muggy breeze rooting forever in his mind's eyes.

After pulling into her driveway and shutting off the engine, he considered his options. He didn't know whether he should ask her on another date now or walk her to her door and ask there. Even three years later and eight thousand miles away in a war zone, the memory still made his hands clammy and moist. He wondered if he might be able to sneak a first kiss or hope for one on a possible second date when she asked if this was all he had planned for the night. He said he hoped to walk her to the front door. She let go of his hand and started opening her door, the look in her eyes telling him that she would love that.

He remembered how the doors creaked shut the way they had that night, and he walked her along the sidewalk, hand in hand with Sara. The yellow light bathed them as she took his hand and stopped on her porch. Joe's heart pounded the walls of his chest, and he felt as if he were drowning in doubt. He bit the bullet and forced himself to ask her if she would like to go out again sometime. Fireworks exploded in his mind when she said, "Yes, I'd like that."

Joe squeezed the covers in the hotel room the way he squeezed his date's hand before he released it. Moving his hand between her arm and waist, he pulled Sara close for the good night kiss he had hoped against hope to give before he left that night. He still felt her arms resting around his neck and on his shoulders as she closed her eyes and felt his left hand lifting her chin before their lips met in their first kiss. Joe tasted her cherry lip balm and wintergreen breath mint from the movie theater. He felt her lean into him on her tip-toes and her soft chest against his in the kiss that lasted only a moment before it broke. Opening his eyes when she opened hers, he knew something fantastic had occurred under the Iowa night sky. Joe's heart skipped, and it thumped erratically when he lowered her from her tiptoes and said something along the lines of thanking her and stumbling over how he would call her the next day. He wanted to get out his of bed in Baghdad and skip around the room just like he wanted to do while walking back to the car. Turning around every three steps, he waved goodnight to her in his memory.

Joe's heart and soul contentedly put his mind and body to sleep in a land far from his home. He heard Sara whispering her love from across an ocean, then slipped into sleep.

Chapter Nine

Baghdad, Iraq
Thursday, January 10th, 2005, 0015 hours,
9 hours ahead of Dyersville, IA:

The air in the room pressed in on him, completely still, punctuated only by sounds of two soldiers recharging their batteries. Alien noises, from the city that lay in wait outside the hotel, tried to break through the closed plate glass windows on the eastern wall. Darkness filled the room. Light crept under the curtains to light the edges of the blankets that covered SGT Busch. Black weapons shone darkly, ready to be picked up to defend their owners' lives. A drip of water fell from the showerhead in their bathroom and plinked off the tub floor.

Joe rested on his side soundly asleep with his knees bent slightly and one arm uncovered. His exhausted mind worked spells inside his head and made him roll over. His eyes darted back and forth under shut eyelids while they played a subconscious movie of one forgotten dream after another. A deep breath ended one dream and began the last one he would have for the night.

His mind traveled across expanses of ocean and across America's heartland to his home. A light haze covered the familiar farmyard under an open, blue sky, and an unfamiliar black car drove past the barn raising a small cloud of dust as it moved down the gravel path to the road. Joe walked across the front lawn and past the giant maple trees full of green leaves. His parents standing under the tree looked broken hearted. What was wrong? The entire farm, usually full of roosters crowing and sounds of cattle, was completely void of all sound.

His mother cried silently on her husband's chest while Joe tried to read his father's lips. He yearned to understand what happened and fight through the silent fog.

The comforting arms of his father around his wife's shoulders silenced the tears that fell. Sue turned away from her husband to look directly at Joe as he walked past them. Joe ached to stop and say hi, but his legs wouldn't stop walking across the short, green grass. His mother's heart tried to speak to him, but he couldn't hear anything through the fog that covered the ground between the mother and son. His legs could not stop walking until he was at the base of the white flag pole in his mother's rose garden.

He felt the deep, powerful, and raw urge grow from deep inside his soul where his love of his country and patriotism grew. Acknowledging what the feeling meant, he reached out to hold the cord on the pole and lower the family's flag. He unclasped the plastic loops from the brass grommets and held the cloth of red and white stripes in his hand. His eyes filled with salty tears, and a single one rolled down his cheek and fell onto the blue field of white stars. Sue continued to stare at, and through her son, as though she was looking at a ghost.

Joe wrapped himself in the flag and felt the weight of his decision to serve and the sacrifices he might have to make, resting on his shoulders.

Sue tried to say, "I love you, Joe."

He wanted to shout to her, to make himself heard, to let her know that everything would be fine. He wanted to run to her and hold her close and let her cry on the flag that wrapped around him. His love for the woman who raised him flooded his heart and soul as another tear fell from his cheek onto the colors of his country.

His feet were glued in place until he mouthed to Sue "I love you, Mom. Everything is okay now. You don't have to worry anymore."

Joe pulled the colored cloth tighter around his shoulders and turned away from Sue to hide the tears that fell non-stop. He began to walk slowly away from his parents and into the fog that held the countryside of his home and dream.

Joe's eyelids fluttered and opened, a sense of wonder displayed for a moment. Then he closed them and slept peacefully.

Chapter Ten

Baghdad, Iraq
Thursday, January 10th, 2005, 0315 hrs,
9 hours ahead of Dyersville, IA:

The alarm beeped through Joe's ears following his unsettling dream. His eyes opened to a room engulfed in darkness, a rectangle of light coming from the door leading to the patio that overlooked the city outside his room. As he lay on his back, Joe listened to Greg outside talking to the guards stationed directly below their room. A whiff of secondhand smoke wafted into the room and completely awakened the Joe.

After stripping the covers back and getting out of bed, he stretched his arms over his head and yawned mightily. His thoughts went to the 36 hours that lay in front of him before he would be able to sleep once more. Hoping to catch a short nap after his patrol today, he pulled the pack of smokes from his trousers, which lay in a heap, and made his way out to the balcony.

"Morning, dude."

"What's new?

"Not too much, bro`. If you hadn't woken up when you did, I was going to pull you out of bed and shut your clock off."

"Thanks for looking out for me. I'm sure you had my best interests at heart."

"I actually about woke you up with that last dream you had. From what I saw, it looked pretty intense."

Joe recalled the dream and thought for a moment.

"That it was, my friend. That it was. Hey, lemme' see your lighter real quick."

Greg flipped his Zippo into the air for Joe to catch. The yellow and white light from the city that rested beneath them glinted off the brushed, stainless steel cover. After watching it fall into his hand, Joe popped the cover open and rolled the flint under his thumb. He watched the flame grow before being sucked into the tip of his own cigarette and snapped the cover shut.

"Thanks. How long have you been up?"

"It's what...0300 now?"

"It's more like oh-too damn early."

"If it's still too damn early, then the past two hours haven't happened yet, and you still have some sleep remaining."

Joe drew on his cigarette. "Gotcha. What does the brass have planned for you this morning?"

"Quick Reaction Force until you guys get back from your patrol, and then we are going for a mail run to the airport."

Joe smiled intently. "Lucky bastards, you should be able to catch some good shuteye. Last I knew we were supposed to roll out around 3:45 or so."

"Yeah, I am hoping to."

"Well, thanks for the light again. I got to get goin' here and at least shave," Joe said flipping his smoke off the balcony. He started to walk back in to get ready for the day.

"Have fun on the sightseeing tour," Greg said sarcastically.

"Always do, man. We always do."

Joe made his way over to the bathroom, kicking his pants into the small room on his way. He stripped his boxers off and pulled his trousers up to his waist leaving the waist hanging open. After turning on the water, he lathered his face with shaving cream. After methodically shaving, he rinsed off the left-over cream, opened the case holding his toothbrush, and pulled it out to put toothpaste on the bristles. Back and forth, up and down, he scraped the morning cigarette breath off. He walked out to pull a clean, brown t-shirt from his laundry bag.

He returned into the bathroom and spit a mouthful of white foam into the stained, porcelain sink. Pulling the cap from the deodorant stick, he rubbed his armpits. His armpits still stung from the prior day when he used the wrong end of the stick in a slumbery mistake and scratched the hell out his underarms. He put the stick with the cap on back into his shaving kit bag and finished brushing his teeth. Scraping his tongue, he made sure he scraped far enough back to lightly trigger the gag reflex to cough up some cigarette tar from his throat and spit a last mouthful of brownish white foam into the drain.

After pulling the clean t-shirt on, he tucked it into the open waist of the brown and tan camouflage trousers. Joe flipped the light in the bathroom off and returned to the foot of his bed. He felt around in the laundry bag, found two socks, and hoped that they were a pair before pulling them onto his feet. The boots he wore yesterday sat where he kicked them off a few short hours before. In the darkness, he inserted his pants into the canvas boots and tightly laced them. He tied them and tucked the boot strings into the side by his ankles before blousing his pants.

The routine almost complete, he slung the desert camouflage shirt around his shoulders and felt his arms sliding through the sleeves. Joe rose and buttoned the shirt and took his weapon along to put his body armor on. He left the front hanging open as he routed the rifle's sling through the d-ring on his right shoulder.

Before he left the room, he went back to his bed and knelt down to pick up the box containing the proposal and surrogate engagement ring. Holding the box close to his heart and whispering a quick prayer, the Memorare, he stood and snagged his helmet and let his friend know he was leaving for the day. "Hey, Greg, I'm out man. I'll probably see you later sometime."

"Is that a date?"

"Only if you want it."

"I knew you just wanted my body. I was looking for something more serious."

"I gotta` get going, man. This relationship is moving way too fast for me."

"Peace out, Bro."

Joe shut the door behind him and sauntered down the hall and called the elevator. He could hear his men up and moving around in their own rooms. Johnson strolled down the hall past him wearing nothing but a towel slung over his shoulder.

"Morning, Sergeant," he called out in a mood too chipper for this early in the morning, but Joe would play along with the joke.

"Taking ole Richard out for a morning swing, huh, Johnson."

"He likes the cool morning air but hates the cold water in my room. I'm showering in Reed's room."

"Are you sure that's all you're planning on doing. I heard you two making sweet love last night," Joe said allegedly referring to the free spirited specialist monkeying his way down the hall.

"We were going to invite you and SGT Forrester, but you tried to take advantage of us last time."

The elevator doors slid open, and Joe stepped inside the elevator and held the door open to have the last word in the messed up conversation. "It's not our fault. You guys invited the gerbils."

"That's disgusting, Sergeant. Have a good day," Johnson said opening the door to Reed's room and disappearing.

The elevator doors clanged shut and started to rise to the sky level of the hotel. He leaned against the doors and watched the lights of the city twinkle while he rode in silence.

The elevator slid effortlessly to a stop at the summit before the doors glided open with a barely audible squeak. Joe stepped into the shadowy corridor. The Command Quarters, or CQ, offered the only light at the very end to the left. He strolled down the hallway through the shadows and into the office that once served as a bar. He could hear Parker's voice on the radio performing radio checks from 19 stories below. The wall to the left held a map of Baghdad that measured eight feet by eight feet. Their unit's sector was highlighted in yellow with different streets named after the larger cities in America and the board game Monopoly. San Francisco, Chicago, and Dallas ran east and west. Those streets were separated by three city blocks and intersected by the north and south running streets Pittsburgh, Miami, and New York.

Busch walked over to the mailbox and set his proposal box gingerly on top of the stack of letters from the men to their families and friends back home in America. The young private on duty that morning looked over at him from behind the converted bar. Joe turned away from him and walked over to the map wall where the coffee pot waited. He wondered how long the coffee might have been brewing before he got there.

Picking up a Styrofoam cup and pouring himself some murky black goodness, he studied the mission route that was highlighted in blue. He looked down for a packet of sugar and one of powdered creamer. When the cup that usually held them was discovered to be void of any sugar, Joe made up his mind that some poor Meal Ready to Eat, MRE, would be ravaged for it grainy packet of sweetness before his coffee cooled down too much.

"HEY, CQ!"

"What's up, Sergeant?"

"Where the fuck's the sugar? You better come up with some in the next minute before life gets real rough for you. It's early in the morning, and I don't want to ruin your day this early."

"Roger, Sergeant, I'll find some." The Private almost tripped over himself as he rushed to rape an MRE in the supply room.

He reappeared in the office with the creamer and sugar in hand in less than the blink of an eye.

"That's more like it, turd."

"Roger, Sergeant. Thank you for alerting me to the fact that we weren't catering to your sweet tooth."

"You getting cocky?"

"Negative, Sergeant!" the private answered.

"That's good, because I already seen too much of that this morning when I was waiting for the elevator."

"Johnson's hot water run out again?"

"Yeah, and he still likes to walk around in the buff swinging Richard everywhere."

"He got me good the other morning, too, Sergeant"

"I wasn't asking for your stories, turd. Answer that radio. My guy is downstairs waiting for your deaf ass to answer back." The private's attempts at conversation were trying Joe's last nerves. He was a new kid who reported to the unit just a week prior to deploying and somehow snagged a ticket to come along on their trip. Busch had not taken the time to learn the kid's name yet and didn't intend to learn it until he learned his right place at the bottom of the unit's food chain.

He continued to study the route of the patrol as he stirred the cream and sugar into his cup of coffee that cooled in his hands. The fiery red highlight that blocked out the section of the city to be patrolled stared back at him. The intelligence brief was posted in a plastic sheet protector next to the map on the wall. Busch sipped the black coffee and took a long glance at the brief.

After he read that the status of the city had not changed overnight, he velcroed the front of his body armor shut. He adjusted the plate in the front so that it wouldn't rub on the St. Michael medal dangling on a chain around his neck. He felt the back pocket for his identification tags; the thin metal tags rested peacefully in the bottom of the pocket. His fingers traced the beady chain from the opening to the belt loop through which the chain was routed.

His mind fresh with the mission information to brief his men that awaited him downstairs, he pivoted and left the CQ office, entering the shadowy hallway. The brass box of the elevator waited patiently for him to step inside and take a ride. Joe stepped into the brass cubicle of light, punched the bottom button, and waited.

His gut jumped a little when the elevator descended down the long chasm lined on one side with lights of the city. Joe leaned against the railing on the wall by the buttons and reached into his cargo pocket for his smokes. The pack opened in his pocket, and his fingers pulled a cigarette out of the pack, then closed the cardboard lid. The elevator kept falling floor after floor. At the mezzanine level, Busch cupped the front of his helmet placing it on his head. The cigarette dangled from his mouth, and an unfastened chinstrap swung back and forth as the ride ended and he stepped into the hotel lobby. "You John Wayne, Meesta Serjunt," the Iraqi desk clerk commented.

"Mr. Wayne would only be as fortunate to look as good as I do," Joe said walking past the porcelain statuette in the center of the lobby. The nude statue stood proudly displaying her feminine body over a shimmering pool of crystal blue water.

The lobby was coated in marble... marble floors, marble walls, marble desks, and even some furniture was carved of the stone. Brass was inlaid between the marble tiles on the floor and walls while the desk and fountain were each mated snugly together.

"Salaam Malaku, Meesta. Have a safe patrol."

"I'll try, buddy. Hope to see you this afternoon."

The Iraqi hotel staff was glad to have the American unit staying in their luxurious lodge. It meant that their security was guaranteed as long as the Americans laid their heads down on their pillows.

Joe headed for the front doors and pulled his lighter out as he pushed the door open. The smell of the Tigris River that flowed less than two blocks away hit the man like a shovel in his nose. Odors of trash and sewage in the streets mixed with the body odor of two million Iraqis. He stopped for a moment to look up at the black sky filled with barely visible stars and light his dangling cigarette.

A trail of smoke floated from the man's nostrils after his first drag. He took another puff and held it deep in his lungs while he stepped down the stairs and into the driveway of his home away from home. He could see his men in the parking lot finishing their jobs of prepping the vehicles. Busch walked nonchalantly across the cracked pavement and stopped at the hood of the first armored HMMWV.

Finn stood in the hatch of the tan vehicle. The diesel engine purred under a fiberglass hood, and its warm exhaust evaporated in the morning air. The truck next to it was also running while the team's medic, Doc Jones, checked his medical supplies on the hood. Bandages and combat lifesaver bags were laid out in neat rows while he methodically checked every single one for the correct elements.

Joe's team consisted of Specialists Robert Parker and Alan Finn, PFC's Juan Zapatto and Rob Taylor, and a black Sergeant named Gaius Reed. Finn would gun the M2 .50 caliber machine gun already mounted in the turret of the lead truck. Parker always drove for SGT Busch, and he knew how his Sergeant liked him to drive.

Doc Jones knew he would be riding in the second truck. Zapatto had already mounted his M249 squad automatic weapon in the turret of that truck which Taylor would drive and SGT Reed would command. The morning air around the teams was interspersed with the chuckles of the men ribbing each other. SGT Reed met with Joe several paces short of the trucks out of earshot of the two teams.

"Morning, Big B. How's it hanging?" Reed asked.

"Kind of short, stubby and to the left. I think he's hibernating, bro," Joe said.

"That's too bad. What's the route looking like?"

"Well, let's see..." Busch pulled another drag on his cigarette before continuing. "We are going to roll down to New York first, sit there until the sun comes up, and keep an eye on the marketplace. Then we're just going to do some sightseeing around the Pennsylvania area where the guards on the roof saw some shooting a few hours ago. How's that sound?"

"Sounds like another day in paradise."

Joe dragged on his cigarette. "Did you watch these guys prepping the vehicles?"

"Yeah, we took care of that just before you got out here. How's the coffee this morning?"

"That piece of shit turd up there didn't have any cream and sugar. Almost had to make life rough for him."

"He is a cocky, little bastard, isn't he?"

Joe smiled. "Reminds me of you a few months ago."

"You're a riot when you don't get some sugar in your system. What lit the fuse on your tampon?"

"Didn't sleep for shit last night, man. This bullshit of only sleeping every two days is starting to get to me. I'm getting low on smokes, too."

"Me, too. Anyways, radio checks are complete. The fifty and SAW are locked and loaded on trucks with full fuel tanks."

"Sounds like you're on top of it. Get the guys over here for the brief."

Reed turned around and hollered at the group of paratroopers standing around the front of the second truck. "Hey, quit jerkin' each other off and get over here for the brief."

Busch finished his smoke and took the last sip of his cold coffee while watching the five men amber over to the sergeants. He crushed the cherry under the toe of his boot and dropped the empty cup to the ground. The light morning breeze blew the cup into a semicircle on the blacktop before it rolled away, finding a quiet place to rest next to a storm drain.

"Gaw' mawning, gentlemen, hope you got some sleep last night...." Busch looked around at the teams that waited patiently to hear the mission brief.

"All right now, Parker, you're driving me. Finn, you know you're gunning the fifty. Doc, you ride with SGT Reed in the second truck. Zapatto, you know you're manning your SAW, and Taylor is driving the second truck. Any questions so far. I know there's one thing on everyone's mind, but gentlemen, that pussy is 8000 miles away. Get her out of your head."

Reed took over the brief. "We're going to sit at the market until sometime around sun up. Then we're going to do some sightseeing around the Pennsylvania area. Taylor, how do we react to contact?"

"Depends on what it is and how bad the trucks are. If it's an IED and we can still drive, we get out of the kill zone and gain fire superiority. If the first truck gets hit and disabled, I push it out of the kill zone, and we establish security. If we get hit, we kick some ass and fight through the ambush."

"Good answer. Everyone understand that?"

The squad nodded.

"Parker, what do we do if someone catches a hot one?" Joe asked.

"We gain fire superiority and control of the situation before tending to any wounded."

"You're the man, dude"

"You know it, Sergeant."

"Let's mount up. We are rolling out in five mikes." Joe gave the command, confident that the trucks and men were ready to kill first and ask questions later. "One more thing guys, we know we're the best damn paratroopers in this city, so let's act like it. We're trying to keep the peace; we only kick ass when they fire first."

"HOOAHH!" came the excited answers.

The group broke up, and the soldiers put their game faces on while walking to their stations. Joe strode to his seat on the passenger side of the lead truck. He opened the armored door and let it hang open as he sat down with one leg hanging out. He grabbed the black handset. The handset was connected to the green radio with a glowing face displaying the frequency over a conglomeration of black buttons.

"Cobra Seven One, Cobra Seven One, this is Cobra One One actual, radio check, over." He performed the last communication test before setting out on the patrol. The truck shimmied slightly under his butt from the eight cylinder diesel engine that purred under the hood. He waited for the response from CQ office and the radio watch operator.

"Cobra One One, this is Cobra Seven One. I have you Lima Charlie. How do you read this station?"

"Cobra Seven One, I have you loud and stupid. Just a reminder, you better have some coffee waiting for us when we get back. Over." Joe snapped the button.

"Roger, One One actual, this is Seven One, out."

Joe stepped out of the tan beast with the enormous machine gun in the turret to watch his squad get mounted in their trucks. Parker was already sitting in the driver's seat. His weapon lay across the center console with the muzzle in front of his body armor and against the door. His window was rolled down, his elbow resting comfortably allowing him to drive with his other hand.

Finn's large frame stretched from 6'2" all the way to the ground, and his lanky leg stepped on the brush guard on the front of the truck as he pulled himself up to scale over the hood. He stepped over the windshield and clunked his way around the turret over Joe's and Parker's heads. Finn dropped through the hatch and leaned against the back of the turret before unlocking the swivel on the fifty. He clicked the turret loose and spun it in a complete revolution to double check that he could maintain 360 degree coverage.

SGT Reed watched his own truck go through the same motions. It was routine, but at the same time, every man could feel the adrenaline begin to flow. Even though they slept in the middle of the enemy's capital, they would venture out this morning to move in the enemy's presence. Reed raised his arm and gave a thumb up to let Joe know that he was ready to roll out the gate. "Let's do this shit and get back here soon, SGT Busch!" Reed said.

Joe chambered a round in his rifle and slid into his seat. "Lock and load, boys. Let's go shopping."

"It's about time, Sergeant. I need a new purse to match the dress I bought last week at the market," Finn hollered through the hatch.

"Sounds like a plan, Klinger. Let's go, Parker. You know the route."

Joe picked up the hand mike, pressed the button, and held it to his ear. "Cobra Seven One, Cobra Seven One, this is Cobra One One actual, over."

"Go ahead One One."

"Roger, Seven One, be advised that I am leaving the hotel at 0400 with two victors and seven personnel. We are en route to the marketplace. How copy, over?"

"I copy leaving the hotel at zero four hundred with two victors and seven motivated paratroopers en route to the market. Over."

"That's a good copy, Seven One. This is One One actual, out.

Chapter Eleven

Baghdad, Iraq
Thursday, January 10th, 2005, 0402 hours,
9 hours ahead of Dyersville, Iowa:

Joe set the hand mike on top of the radio mount while Parker wove his way through the vehicle barriers on the snake path out of the hotel's entrance. Joe recognized the guards manning the gate and waved a salute to them as they passed under the raised bar. Parker hung a left turn immediately after leaving the gate and drove down the alley way. At the end of the alley way, he genuflected a stop only long enough to spot a break in the Baghdad traffic and gunned the horses under the hood. The turbocharger whinnied its approval as the vehicle streaked across three lanes of traffic, hopped over the median, and turned left again into the northbound traffic.

Both trucks swerved and dodged traffic during the fifteen minute commute to the marketplace. Red lights meant nothing, and three Iraqis driving rusty taxis lost a bumper or gained a dent when they failed to get out of the way. The marketplace was completely filled with early morning shoppers gathering around burn barrels to keep warm.

Trucks loaded heavy with vegetables pulled into the plaza and stopped next to their produce stands. Bushels of green lettuce and various fruits were unloaded in minutes and left in a pile for the individual vendors to sort and stack. A small herd of fifty various brown, tan, and white sheep strolled past the produce and stole a nibble of fresh greenery on their way to a neighboring field.

A local citizen could buy everything he or she would need in one trip to this market. An American could classify the court as a miniature Super Wal-Mart. Shoppers on the prowl for early morning deals on shoes, washing machines, milk, or meat still on the hoof could buy the world in a single trip. The best part of the deal depended on how well a shopper could haggle the shop owners on their prices. Cut-throat competition occurred here simply because a bargain hunter could walk a few more steps and play one merchant against his or her competitor.

Kids with trays of cigarettes and warm sodas waited for the two truck convoy to pull up and park. Joe gave the order to park and to assume a defensive posture with the drivers parking for an easy escape route where they wouldn't be blinded by the rising sun. The peddling kids swarmed the vehicles when Joe opened his door and stretched his legs.

His finger covered the trigger, and his thumb applied slight pressure to the selector lever ready to switch from safe to semi automatic. Joe's reflexes stood on guard, and his keen eyes surveyed the hundreds of early morning risers. He waited for one to make the wrong move and threaten him or his men. Several of the civilians walking past him caught his probing eyes and looked away as soon as they were caught looking at the Americans.

The residents of this neighborhood knew these men were called paratroopers, and they meant nothing but business. The parts of the city that knew the patrols of these battle-hardened men also knew peace like they never knew before the war. America grew tall and strong men that wore armor that stopped bullets. Iraqis knew that these men fought alongside each other indifferent to color or creed. The patch on their shoulder with double A's in a black circle identified these brave men who fought with the audacity known only to the radical extremists of their own culture.

Joe spied the kid that sold him cigarettes for a great price. "Hey, Skinny, come here."

A tiny five or six-year-old kid, dirty from never knowing a bath and always living on the streets, recognized his American friend and his assigned moniker. His bare feet slapped the grimy pavement as he ran over to the tall paratrooper from the other side of the world.

"Meesta, you want good deal on cheegarettes?"

"Sure, Skinny, how much?"

"For me American friend, two pack Miami…one dolla," he pitched holding up two packs and one finger.

"Finn, you got me covered?"

"Roger, Sergeant, I got you."

Joe reached back into the truck and grabbed the hand mike on the radio. He stood with his back to the truck and raised CQ on the radio.

"Cobra Seven One, this is Cobra One One."

"This is Seven One. Go ahead One One."

"Hey, roger, we are at the marketplace pulling security, going to talk to a local, and get some Intel. How copy, over?"

The radio squawked back in his ear, "Roger that's a good copy, One One. You're at the marketplace. Let us know when you roll out to check out the Pennsylvania neighborhood."

"I'll do that Seven One. This is One One, out." Joe tossed the handset back into the truck and watched it tumble across the console. "Smoke 'em if you need to, Parker. We're going to be here awhile." He turned back to the anxious street urchin.

Busch squatted down to look the small child in the eyes. "What can I get for two dollars?" Busch held up two American greenbacks. "Can you tell me where the bomb is today?" SGT

Busch knew his friend's intelligence could be relied on better than his Uncle Sam's.

"No bomba today, Meesta."

Busch folded up the two dollars and pretended to put them away into his pocket.

"OK. OK, Meesta, three dolla, and I tell you."

Joe held up the original greenbacks with a third, "Where is it, kid?"

"Over there." Skinny's eyes never left the three precious dollars while pointing toward the Pennsylvania area of Joe's sector.

"How far over there?"

"By mosque, lots of shooting there last night." Skinny's eyes darted around, his nervousness showing through his bravery like a beacon from a light house.

"Are you sure, Skinny?"

"110 per chent. Do you want cheegattes or no, Meesta?" His feet started to dance during the mini interrogation.

"Yeah, I want the cigarettes." Busch handed the three dollars over for his two packs of coffin nails.

The deal complete, Skinny turned around and ran back to his friends to show off his hard earned American currency.

Joe stood up slowly and looked around him, taking in the eyes of the middle-aged men that stood on the edge of the crowd. He walked over to SGT Reed and motioned for him to lower his window.

"Find anything out, Big B?"

"Skinny said there will be a bomb down by Pennsylvania. The rooftop guards said there was a bunch of celebratory firing last night around the mosque that's down there, too." He peeled the cellophane from his new pack of smokes, opened the box, and pulled a smoke out.

"You thinking about checking it out later?"

"That's our mission," he said as he lit the cigarette.

"How do you want to do it and when? The sun is already starting to peek over the skyline."

Joe scanned the area and growing crowd in the marketplace and took another drag. "What time do you think we should roll out of here?" he asked.

"I'm getting uncomfortable already just sitting here. You know me. I like to burn fuel driving around."

"Me, too, I feel like a sitting duck. Let's wait half-an-hour and keep an eye on anyone we think is interesting here."

"Good enough."

"I'll let you know when I give the OK to roll out," Joe said and left his fellow sergeant sitting there with his elbow on the window and marched back to his truck.

Joe sat down in the truck with the door open to let some of the diesel exhaust to blow in along with his own noxious exhaust from the cigarette in his lips. The chin strap on his helmet was beginning to scratch his hairless chin and begged to be unfastened.

"Hey, Finn, I want you to keep that big fucker pointed in the general direction of the crowd."

"Already watching them through the sights, Sergeant."

"That's why I love having you on the fifty."

Joe's cigarette was edging closer to burning the filter between his fingers. One last pull of smoke deep into his lungs, and he flicked it in the direction of the crowd. He held the smoke in the recesses of his airways and savored the taste in his mouth. The skyline in the distance was highlighted by the rising sun and glared off the desert floor that surrounded the city. A pink tint littered the rising particles of smog and dust in the filthy city. Joe blew the smoke from his lungs through his nose so he could relish every morsel of dying slowly and watched the swirling trails evaporate.

The early morning traffic began to back up. Taxis and cars voiced their discontent through beeps and honks. The pink sky and air began to turn a light tan, gradually being congested with smog and dust from the desert edges. Burn barrels lit hours ago to keep insomniac vendors warm smoldered to their last coals. Trails of smoke delicately wagged, disappearing into the early haze of daylight.

"OK, Parker, let's get going and make a circle around Pennsylvania and pick a spot to sit there for awhile."

"Roger, Sergeant."

"Finn, you ready to roll up there?" Joe hollered over his shoulder.

"I will be by the time we drive away."

"Good deal."

Picking up the hand mike, Joe began, "Cobra Seven One, this is Cobra One One, over."

"Go ahead One One."

"Hey, be advised we're leaving the marketplace in route to do a few racetracks around Pennsylvania before settling down in a good spot."

"Roger, I'll log you leaving the market at 0700."

"That's a good copy. One One, out."

SGT Reed gave his thumbs up from his truck to let Joe know he was ready.

"Let's do it, Parker. Get on New York and cut left a block before we get to PA. I want to drop in before the traffic circle."

Parker dropped the transmission into drive and honked the horn once before gunning the engine into the traffic. The brush guard swiped the side of a banged up Mercedes Benz when the armored truck cut into and across traffic into the south bound lanes. Finn swung the hatch around to aim into the oncoming traffic practically begging someone to make a move.

The engine roared as the turbocharger kicked in and whined more ponies into the wheels driving the truck. SGT Reed stayed close on the lead truck's shadow, too close for any vehicle to squeeze between the convoy. Thick, black tires pounded the cracked pavement, bouncing over potholes and debris in the road. A manhole cover clunked quickly as the wheels ran directly over it.

Parker jerked the wheel, crossed three lanes and into the last side street before their anticipated target. The narrow street, barely larger than an alley way, was lined with two door sedans of different colors and cracked windshields. Buildings on each side towered over the speeding convoy as it roared down the path. A few local residents looked out the window of a coffee shop at the hustling pair of trucks. One coffee drinker raised a friendly wave at the patrol as it sped past before any of the soldiers could return the salute.

The convoy neared the point in the route to New York where Joe specified to get off and cut into a back passageway to avoid a chokepoint ahead. Shattered windows glared with unblinking and hollow eyes at the Americans trespassing on streets they weren't meant to be on.

Parker screeched his truck's tires through the right turn down an even shorter alley and barreled smoothly onto Pennsylvania a block shy of the traffic circle. The racetrack maneuver began with both trucks in formation, the second directly in the shadow of the lead truck, and gunning their engines into the inside track of the circle. Gunners Finn and Zappy rotated their machine guns in a wide one hundred and eighty degree arc of security in their assigned sectors as the trucks bellowed into the unavoidable bottleneck of the traffic roundabout.

Joe and SGT Reed were slammed against the doors of their HMMWV's as the trucks battled around the traffic circle before exiting into the eastbound lanes of Pennsylvania. Horses under the hood, already pushed to their limits, strained against their reins even stronger. Turbochargers whimpered their protest and slapped the harnesses on the ponies' backs. Blocks of the city streaked past in a blur while traffic attempted to get out of the patrol's way before losing a bumper.

The deafening noise shattered past less than a blink of a heartbeat after the blazing flash. A brutal concussion wave swamped the truck and slammed Finn down through the hatch leaving his machine gun waving wildly in the air. A blinded Parker held the wheel straight and prepared to drive through the giant fireball engulfing the road. Stunned, Joe reached for the hand mike.

"Cobra Seven One, Cobra Seven One!" he shouted into the handset while they passed through the fireball. "This is Cobra One One! We have survived an IED on the south side of Pennsylvania."

Finn, bleeding lightly from his cheek, climbed back up through the hatch, rotated his weapon from safe to fully automatic, and scanned the road ahead of the patrol. "Enemy two o'clock. Three AK's in sight. More at nine o'clock!"

"Open fire, Finn. Open fire *NOW!*"

The fifty chattered loudly, sending tears of lead screaming through the air at the insurgents who ducked behind walls and into alleys.

"SERGEANT, THE STEERING IS GONE."

"FUCK!" Busch shouted into the radio as he felt the truck coasting to a stop. "REED, WE HAVE A DEAD TRUCK! HIT US HARD, AND GET US OUT OF THE KILL ZONE!"

Resisted bullets bounced off the glass.

Plink, plink. The bullet proof windshield spider webbed from stopping two enemy bullets.

"COBRA SEVEN ONE! COBRA SEVEN ONE, WE HAVE A DEAD TRUCK. GET THE QRF OUT HERE NOW. WE ARE TAKING ENEMY FIRE."

"Roger, One One, QRF is already on their way."

Reed's truck slammed into the tailgate and started to push the wounded truck as fast as possible. Finn kept slinging lead downrange in five to seven shot bursts.

The second flash blinded both trucks and slammed a chuck of concrete into Finn's body armor, knocking him into the back of the hatch and cracking one of the ribs on his left side. The fireball swallowed both trucks, singeing the hair on Zapatto's neck under his helmet. His face was saved by staying in his sector and facing away. Doc pulled his nine millimeter pistol out of the holster on his leg and lowered his window. Shots rang out from the back of the second truck as Doc fired on the enemy. An Iraqi dropped to the ground, his brains spilling from the hole in his turban.

"SEVEN ONE, SEVEN ONE," the radio crackled in Busch's truck with the sound of Reed's voice. "We have two dead trucks. TELL QRF TO HURRY THE FUCK UP! Sergeant, you copy that?"

"Roger, man, I got you. Let's do this shit. Follow my lead," Joe said into the hand mike. "Parker, you better be able to shoot because we have to get out of the truck."

"Reed." Joe gained his composure and spoke into the radio as rounds plinked off the armor of the truck. "You have the back half of security. Stay behind your door and listen to the radio after you get out. Keep the gunners in the hatch unless the truck starts on fire. Use these other cars as cover. Me and Parker will take the lead half of security. We have to kill these fuckers before they pick us off one by one."

"Let's do this!" Reed replied.

"SEVEN ONE, be advised we are going to the ground to kill these fuckers," Joe informed the command. Parker was the first to exit the truck. He popped his door open and rolled to the ground. He crawled to the cover of a dead Dodge Omni with the driver inside leaning to his left, a piece of shrapnel sticking sharply out of his chest. His heart was already shredded.

Not waiting for a reply from CQ, Joe opened his door and stepped into the incoming fire. A round zipped past his ear as he ran to the left front of the truck and slid behind a burning car. He looked behind him and saw Reed crouching behind his door and firing round after round into a group of attackers. Doc leaned against another vehicle, reloading his pistol. Both machine guns were opening on anything that moved. Joe stood up, switched from safe to semi, raised his rifle, and picked out a target in one smooth motion.

The rifle bucked slightly, sending its first round into the chest of an old man held in front of an attacker. The second round was mailed when the elder crumpled to the ground leaving the body of the enemy in clear view. The weapon drooped in the enemy's hand as the round buried itself in the Iraqi's shoulder.

Busch listened to the zip of lead pass around him. The world was eerily silent. The only sounds were the barking of battle dogs fighting for their lives. The outnumbered squad began to turn the tide of the fight. The fifty began to take buildings down under the control of the excellent aim of Finn. The second machine gun squeaked out slugs one after another mowing down the enemy to the rear and slicing open windshields.

Joe caught the sight of a second story window being thrown open with a long pointed spear sticking out as the shutters slammed against the wall.

"FINN. Zapatto. RPG ELEVEN O'CLOCK!" Busch shouted with all his might. "EVERYONE GET DOWN. NOW." Joe raised an arm and motioned for Parker to get down.

The rocket propelled grenade belched steam and smoke as Joe began to lower his arm. A round fired from an AK47 on the side of the road found its true home. It pierced Joe's t-shirt at the bottom of the sleeve. It split the skin and shattered the rib bone which was knocked out of place years ago by a cow.

The RPG streaked over the top of both trucks as Finn swung the turret around and lit up the insurgents' nest.

A burning sensation filled Joe's chest, and his arm fell before he crumpled to the ground. His helmet banged off the ground. His weapon lay by his side as he struggled to roll over. Joe tried to cough the burn out of his torso. Blood stained his lips and flew from his nose onto his body armor.

Joe squirmed over to the cover of the iron horse that carried him into battle. His left arm felt like lead as he propped himself against the flat, front tire. Joe reached out with his right hand and pushed his door shut so he could see SGT Reed.

"Busch!" Reed screamed when he saw his friend on the ground with blood on his chin. "FUCK! ARE YOU HIT?"

Joe couldn't hear him but could see his lips moving through the din of the firefight. He pulled his right knee up and supported his weapon on top of his knee cap. He made a fist with his right hand and coughed into it, spotting his hands with fresh, bubbling blood. He held it out to Reed and forced his thumb up, letting him know that he was going to be OK.

Reed saw the bloody cough and grabbed the handset.

"SEVEN ONE, SEVEN ONE, WE HAVE A MAN DOWN!"

Chapter Twelve

Sara hesitated at the front door of the farmhouse. Reaching out, she pushed the bell button. The door swung open in seconds.

"Sara, hi! We weren't expecting to see you tonight. How've you been? Come in out of this cold. You'll catch your death. Come in. We're just finishing supper. Have you eaten yet?" Sue, Joe's mother, prattled on with the unannounced arrival of Joe's girlfriend. "Have you talked to Joe at all lately? I don't think that boy ever thinks about writing home to his family, but I'm sure he finds the time to write to you though."

"Hello, Sue. Thanks, but I ate before I came out here. I hope I'm not interrupting anything. Am I?"

"Oh, gracious, no. You know we always have time for you. You look great by the way. There is a glow about you tonight. Did you get your hair cut?"

"Thanks. I got a letter from Joe last week. He said he's doing fine, and everything is going as well as it can over there. But you know if something wasn't going well, he wouldn't tell any of us." Sara laughed lightly as she stepped out of her shoes on the Busch's front porch and followed Sue into the living room. Smells of a supper just eaten greeted Sara, and remnants of a pork roast on a platter still rested on the table surrounded by three dirty plates and silverware with glasses almost emptied of milk.

"Hi, Doug! How you doing? Chores go okay tonight?"

"Hey, Sara. Yeah, chores went fine. We had another calf today. What brings you out to this neck of the woods on a cold night?"

"I have something I need to tell Joe. I was wondering if you could help me because I have a few questions."

"Hey, there, Sara!" Kelly chimed in as she bounced into the room. "How is your break going?"

"Hi, Kelly. Break is going good. You're back in school already, right?"

"Yeah, we started yesterday. I'd stick around, but I just needed to grab another roll to munch on while I work on some stupid homework."

"Kelli, you just ate supper. You don't need anything else to eat now. Get back to doing homework, or you'll get stuck doing dishes," Doug said.

"Let her have something to eat. She's as skinny as a stick and might disappear if she doesn't eat something." Good cop Sue let Kelly have a roll and smiled lovingly at Doug. Kelly bounced out of the kitchen with her blonde ponytail bobbing behind her.

"Anyway, what is it you wanted to talk about again?" Sue asked.

Sara sat down at the kitchen table across from Doug while Sue began to clear the table. She looked around and double-checked that Joe's sister had really gone back up to her bedroom to work on homework. Sara felt her emotions begin to bubble from the tips of her toes and race through her legs, then swell over the secret between her hips and explode in her heart. Sara swallowed and began, "I don't really know how to say this..." Sara waited a second and sighed.

"Are you all right, Honey?" Sue asked as she turned away from the sink and dried her hands on a dishtowel.

"This is just really hard to say. I haven't even told my own family yet."

Sue looked deep into Sara's eyes, "It's all right, Sweetheart," and sat down next to Sara with an arm over her shoulder. "What is it, Darling?"

The arm around her shoulders broke the dam holding back her emotions. Sara blinked once, twice, and then gave up her fight against the deluge. Tears flooded her eyes, and she hid her face behind her hands. Sue's arm squeezed her tightly, and Doug reached across the table and held out a paper towel for Sara to dry her eyes, when she was ready. "I found out this morning."

"Found out what, Sara?" Doug asked while the realization of what Sara was trying to say had dawn on Sue. She wrapped Sara in a great hug and started crying along with her.

Sue squeezed her harder. "We will get through this together. All of us."

"What's going on?" Doug asked again, the idea in his head but not completely ringing out. It felt as if he had a name on the tip of his tongue unable to think of it for his life.

Sara pulled away from Sue for just a second to look at Doug. She grabbed the paper towel and thanked him for it before taking a deep breath.

"How far along," Sue asked between breaths, "are you?" She dabbed at the corners of her eyes and then wiped a tear off Sara's cheek.

"Doug, Sue," Sara looked at each of them. "I'm three months pregnant. Joe is the father, and I have no idea how to tell him." Sara lost her composure and broke down in Sue's arms and sobbed, "He needs to know as soon as possible in case something…something happens."

Chapter Thirteen

Baghdad, Iraq
Thursday, January 10th, 2005, 0734 hours,
9 hours ahead of Dyersville, Iowa:

Greg Forrester and his squad ran through the streets listening to the sounds of the firefight getting closer. His feet pounded the streets, and his armor bounced against his chest. Every man ran with his weapon at the ready, sweeping their muzzles across every person in his way. Sweat ran from their heads, dripping down their backs into the waistband of their pants. The Quick Reaction Force darted along the buildings and storefronts as they made their way toward a raging thunderstorm of bullets.

Forrester wore an earpiece in his ear to listen to the radio chatter from the firefight. He knew that only seven blocks separated the hotel from where the firefight was being fought. He pushed his blood into his lungs and into the muscles in his legs as he drove himself and his men toward the battle raging in his ear.

"Seven One, Seven One," the radio crackled in Greg's ear as it picked up the voices from the fire fight. "We have a man down."

The news that a man was down punched Greg in the solar plexus. He keyed the button on the radio that was attached to his shoulder, "Seven One, this is QRF. Let One One know that we're four blocks away and closing fast. We need to know which way to come into the fight. How copy, over?" Forrester never missed a step while communicating with command.

"QRF, this is Seven One. Be advised; hold up two blocks short on Miami while we get One One back on the mike."

"*Quebec Romeo Foxtrot.* This is One One. I copied your last transmission, over." Sgt Reed's word slammed into Greg's ear.

"Roger One One, this is QRF, be advised. We're one block short of Miami. Which route do you want us to come in on?"

"Hey, man, we need you to cut over to Chicago and come in firing from the east. Be advised, Busch is down. I don't know how badly though. How copy over?"

"That's a good copy. We'll be there in two minutes. Hold out as long as you can."

Greg dropped his hand to his weapon from holding the mike on his shoulder, and he yelled to his point man. "Wilson, hang a right on Miami and cut over to Chicago. Go to Pennsylvania. We're going to come in firing from the east. Everyone else, shoot first and ask questions later." Greg shouted the commands to his squad when they turned down Miami and listened to the fight raging two blocks to their left. "Pick it up to a sprint. SGT Busch is hit and down!"

Greg's own adrenaline streaked through his veins, and his body numbed with the news that his best friend was wounded. He clicked his weapon from safe to semi and covered the trigger well on the rifle. He ran with the squad down the street and covered the men as they rounded the corner onto Chicago.

Greg sucked hard breaths of morning air into his lungs. His heart in his chest battered his ribs with every step.

The squad rolled into a left turn and stepped into the hell of war. Cars and tires burned on the street. The stench of flesh and hair burned by the improvised explosive devices filled the air. Finn fired the fifty in the turret of the lead truck. The muzzle flashes from the massive machine gun sparked through the smoke and dust that clogged the air.

"ALPHA TEAM, TAKE THE LEFT SIDE. BRAVO, WE ARE GOING ON THE RIGHT!"

The squad split in half, and Greg made his way across the debris-strewn street. He ran half-crouched to a doorway and exploded through the entry. The doorway provided him with a chance to see the fight from a safe vantage point and looked down the barrel of his weapon. His team smashed their way past him into the building and stood in a line behind him, ready to follow at the signal.

Greg spotted Parker firing rapidly into an alleyway. His attention was drawn to the southern half of the street where the central shooting was happening. Alpha team tucked itself behind a corner into another alley while enemy rounds chipped at the corner they hid behind.

He swung his weapon onto the group of three insurgents that pinned half of Joe's squad down. As his sights crossed the first shooter's head, it exploded into a crimson mist. Greg swung onto the second shooter and pulled the trigger as the shooter doubled over and three massive holes burst through the front of the enemy's shirt.

He ran through the open door and toward the lead truck and Parker. He darted through the smoke of a burning car. The three members of bravo team leaped through the smoke following Greg into the fight to save a fallen brother.

Joe looked down to see the pool of blood growing on the ground around him. His useless, left arm dangled in its socket just above the wound with no exit hole. He felt his lung filling with blood as though he were drowning with every breath bringing the taste of bubbling blood to his tongue. He spit a small clot from his mouth as he switched his weapon from semi to three round burst.

Three blown-up vehicles separated him from an enemy that turned to fire on Forrester's squad. Joe painfully swung his weapon over and pulled the trigger. As another shooter entered his field of vision, Joe fired another burst into the enemy's chest and watched as the air around the enemy erupted into a burst of pink. The sunlight glinted off the beady drops of blood before they rained onto the street.

Joe realized that he would not make it off this street as his next breath almost didn't happen. He coughed another blood clot free from his windpipe and swallowed it down. He rested his weapon on the shooting perch of his right knee and reached into his pocket for a cigarette. He never felt the need to smoke more than he felt at that moment. The pack opened, and he pulled a smoke out. He held the butt in his lips as he reached again for his lighter.

The beautiful flame danced in front of his face, and he lowered the tip of the cigarette into the heat. He let the lighter fall into the red puddle he sat in. The lighter splashed to the ground, and a small bloody wave rippled out from the center. The lit cigarette dangled from the wounded soldier's lips when he felt the trigger under his fingers once again. Joe pulled a long drag on the coffin nail and smiled at the irony of the situation. Smoke dribbled from his nose while he chose another target and fired.

CRACK POW! CRACK POW! CRACK POW! He paused... then pulled the trigger again. *CRACK POW!* Click.

Joe reached under the weapon to release the spent magazine. The black, banana-shaped magazine bounced off his body armor and clinked to a stop in his lap. He took another drag and breathed out, tasting the bloody smoke that stained his taste buds and lips. He raised his right hand to the filter and pulled it out of his mouth. It rested between his fingers as his strength drained.

His right hand fell to the ground into the seeping puddle. Joe turned his head and looked at the smoldering cigarette on the ground. He listened to the firefight drawing to a close. The mosquitoes of his childhood fantasies of the bullets of battle seemed only to be flying away from him. The world grew completely silent around him, and he took another strained breath.

He looked up to see Doc running toward him and firing at the side of the street. Another breath forced his lung to collapse further. The pressure in his chest grew and the sound of blood pumping through his ears began to fade. He looked down at his hand holding the lit cigarette. Gyrations from his bloody hand announced the shakes were starting to set in. One more breath, one more breath was all he wanted. The edges of his vision clouded over when he felt a hand on his left shoulder. Joe drew in one more breath and willed his body to do one last thing.

Joe looked to the east and raised his eyes to the sun that streamed through the buildings and smoke. A pair of hands grabbed his face. He made out Greg Forrester's face and let out the breath he was holding in his lungs. Greg drifted out of his vision as the sun behind him grew bright. The light burned its way into his heart, and the world remained silent while he looked around. Reality faded into another world half the globe away with his mind completely shattered and hiding in the recesses of his memory.

The green grass crunched under his boots after a tear fell from his cheek and onto the flag that was draped around his shoulders. Joe saw his mother crying in front of the house he'd grown up in. He knew now what his dream meant, and his heart ached through the last beat. He sank into a deep sleep using the last of his breath to tell her, "It's okay, Mom. I'm coming home."

Joe fled the battlefield feeling like a coward leaving his friends to fight a battle in which he thought he died. Totally unsure of where he was, or what just happened, he thought he was in Baghdad, smoking a cigarette, sitting in a pool of his own blood. He remembered feeling the sun becoming extremely hot followed by a horrible vision of his mother crying with him wrapped in his country's flag.

He felt himself floating over a hayfield watching a John Deere 4020 tractor pulling a sickle knocking down the alfalfa to dry in the afternoon sun.

Reality, as muddy as it was to him, set in when he discovered he was witnessing the best day in his life. He watched a three-year-younger version of himself toil away on the family farm through the late afternoon before he took Sara on their first date.

The tractor pulled the haybine through the field of waist-high alfalfa, its driver's mind in various daydreams. The afternoon sun shone brightly down on the green hood of the iron beast through the belching exhaust from the diesel's belly. Grunting and groaning over the hills of the Iowa farm, the tractor drug a rusty and yellow haybine that chewed swath after swath of alfalfa and grasses. The hay was chewed off the stem between two crushing, black rollers dripping with the sweat from the fresh cut feed. Behind the monstrous noise and dust lay a neat windrow of hay to dry in the July sun.

The fifty stopped barking, and an eerie silence covered the street. Finn looked around the battle zone and took in the situation. His forehead dripped blood over the side of his face and down his neck. The broken rib in the right side of his chest stung violently despite the adrenaline. Smoke from the wrecked engine billowed from around the hook obscuring his sight of Joe on the ground.

Parker still stood on the driver's side pulling security with his rifle slowly swinging to the left and the right inviting someone to shoot at him again. Doc and Greg were mumbling incoherent words down by where Joe sat by the front tire. The QRF set up their own security around the disabled vehicles to allow the patrol squad to gather their thoughts and reload their weapons. Finn watched while SGT Reed ran up to Doc and Forrester.

The shirtless young man of seventeen years sat at the wheel of the tractor. His six-feet-four-inch frame slouched in the seat with his arms guiding the process with nimble control of the wheel and throttle. Sweat trickled down his tanned shoulders and over his back. It tasted salty on his lips while he made round after round in the forty acre field. An old, seed corn hat made with a mesh material advertising Pioneer Hybrids covered his head while his mind generated one daydream after another. He squinted his eyes from the reflection of the sun off the hood while watching barn swallows dipping and diving around him, catching the mosquitoes and insects before they had a chance to feast.

He raised his vision from the field to the billowing cloud of dust on the horizon. The familiar shape of his neighbor's farm truck driving down the gravel road caught his attention. Once he made his way to the edge of the forty acres, he held up his hand with the index finger half raised in the country salute between friends, family, and strangers. The driver returned the wave blazing on by the young man on the tractor in the field.

Joe reached out with his right hand and touched the hydraulic controls. Pushing forward on the outermost lever and spinning the steering wheel with his left hand to the right, he pushed on the right brake spinning the tractor and mower on a dime around the corner. His hands spun the wheel straight and reversed the action on the lever to drop the mower back to the ground to begin another trip back across the field.

He began the return trip and slouched back to being comfortable with a small sunburn beginning on his shoulders. Joe let himself be trapped again in his daydreams of being a courageous soldier.

He traveled from the green field in eastern Iowa to far and distant lands in an epic battle where he defended himself against an enemy that far outnumbered him. He didn't have enough ammunition and only one grenade left to get his men and himself out of harm's way. He transformed the buzz of the mosquitoes around him to that of bullets zipping past. The birds in the air became the elusive enemy that he picked off with shot after shot. His sunburn was transformed into the wounds that brought the pain which he fearlessly fought. Thunderous noises erupted around him and drowned out his shouts to his men to stay down.

The sweat on his lips tasted like blood to him, quenching the young man's thirst for gore. He made up his mind that he would live through this battle to fight another day. The battle wound down. The enemy lay on the ground around him and his men as they limped to safety and ended the fight just in time for Joe to turn the corner in the hayfield.

Joe heard a strange noise coming from behind him, and he turned around to see what demon was keeping him from joining his men again in an imaginary war. A beat up red Dodge truck trudged its way over the ruts in the field, honked its horn, and demanded that he stop the tractor. He reached out with his left foot and stepped on the clutch and throttled down the tractor. He shut off the power to the mower as he climbed from his commander's seat and adjusted the bill of his blue, Pioneer hat.

The field of foreign silence seeped into reality as the thoughts of battle slipped from his mind, and he heartily shouted, "Hey, Pops, what's up?"

Doug, Joe's father, already past the half-century mark in age by five years, swung the door of the truck open as the Dodge rolled to a stop. His weather-beaten frame showed the days spent toiling under the hot sun and freezing winters. The thinning hair on his father's head showed more than a few grey strands, making it a salt and pepper combination. His once proud, six-foot-one inch frame had fallen under the six-feet mark a few years before, and a small belly had begun to grow around his middle.

"Just thought you might want a break since you've been out here all day," Joe's father answered.

"Well, I'm almost done here. Another hour will do a lot."

"Big plans for tonight?" Doug asked his son.

"Oh, you know, I might just have another date tonight."

"Didn't you go on one last week?"

"Does that mean I'm not allowed to go on another tonight with a different girl, Dad? I'm a young man, and I have to have some fun."

Doug chuckled to himself, "Yeah, you have a point there. Who's the lucky girl this week?"

"Actually, I think I'm the lucky one tonight. She's a sweetheart. We've been talking a lot lately." Joe's voice trailed off.

"So are you going to tell me her name? Or for that matter, the name of the one you took out last week? I might know her mom from back in the good, old days."

"Her name is Sara. That's all you need to know for now." Joe ducked the part about the girl from the week prior.

"Sara...hmmmm? Would I know her folks?"

"You might, just like I think I might need a drink of water. Got any in the truck?"

"Yeah, I have some water for you in here." The graying-haired man reached into the back of the truck and pulled out a dusty water jug with ice rumbling around under the cap.

Joe flipped the drinking tube up from the top and wiped the dust from it before taking a deep guzzle and inducing an immediate ice-cream headache.

"Where are you taking her tonight?"

"You mean Sara?"

"If that's her real name."

"Funny, Dad, real funny. I was just going to do the whole dinner and a movie. I really liked the movie I saw last week with the guys. I think I'm going to drag Sara along so I can see it again."

Doug laughed and took a swallow or two from the jug. "Just like I did when I was your age?"

"You were the one who gave me the idea. Besides, it was a good movie."

"I don't mean to change the subject, but you got another letter from Iowa State. Any plans or ideas?"

"I'm not sure, Dad. I know I should go to school, but you know what? I'm not sure if it's for me yet. I still have to get through my senior year." Joe wondered if he should tell his dad about his wanting to join the Army. He leaned against the tractor tire and slid down to a squat in the shade.

"Have you thought about anything else besides going to college?"

"He's gone, Reed," Greg said when he stood.

"What do you mean! He's gone?"

"He is fucking dead, man. Gone. He caught a hot one under his armpit into his chest. Fuck, man, what else do you want me to fucking say?"

"Damnit!" Reed cursed. "Is anyone else hurt?"

"I think I broke a rib in the blast," Finn said.

"Anyone else? Parker, you okay?"

"Roger, Sergeant, I'm OK."

"Parker, switch out with Finn so Doc can take a look at him," Reed ordered. "Marius, get the stretcher from the back of our truck and bring it up here. We got to get out of here."

Joe thought back to his daydream. "Yeah, I guess I have."

"What do you mean?"

"I have been thinking about joining the Army. I know you were in the Guard back during Vietnam, and Mom will kill me if I mention that I want to join. But, I just have this feeling. I can't put my finger on it."

"Well, you know I'm behind you. You have always been a little different when it came to that sort of stuff. It won't hurt you at all to think about it. And don't worry about Mom." Doug held the water jug out to Joe sitting in the shade of the tire. "If she gets mad, it'll only be for a little while until she sees what kind of man it will make you."

"Thanks." Joe tipped up the jug and took enough swallows to last the hour.

"You're welcome." Doug wrapped up the talk, took the jug from his son, and offered his hand to help his son get up off the ground. "When you get done, just put the tractor away and grease the mower. Then you're free to have fun on your date tonight. Tell her I said hi, too."

"Thanks for the lift, old man. I'll tell her you said hi. Thanks again for letting me out of chores to see her. You won't regret it." Joe chuckled as he put his hand on the hot tire, "I'll see you in the morning, Dad."

He walked to the tractor and stepped onto the iron beast. The blazingly hot, black, vinyl tractor seat stung his back when he eased into the controls and fired up the old tractor. The black smoke plumed into the sky, and he fed power back to the hungry mower.

He watched with admiration in his eyes as his father began the drive across the field and back to the farm. He released the clutch and began chugging his own path around the field in shrinking paths. He tried to turn the bugs into bullets and birds into enemies again but failed because of a certain girl running through his mind.

The noise of the tractor and mower drowned out Joe's voice as he practiced what he would say to Sara when he picked her up for their first date. Even though he had taken another girl on a date the week before, Joe had been trying to get a date with Sara since he first met her. He really liked her and hoped that something more than just dinner and a movie would develop from this. Joe knew already that a man wasn't supposed to let himself think past the first date nor hope for more than a kiss at the end of the night. His heart picked the locks on his mind, and he thought about how he had asked her out earlier in the week. He hoped she had not seen his knees shaking or the sweat *dampening the palms of his hands. He always dreamed of asking a girl like her out and then having her say "yes" to just a simple date.*

Parker climbed up onto the hood of the truck and helped Finn climb out of the turret. He handed his rifle to Finn and dropped into the hatch behind a machine with a steaming barrel. Finn slowly made his way through the haze over the engine and gingerly lowered himself to the ground. Marius walked over to the group at the front of the truck carrying the stretcher. Doc pulled the smoldering cigarette from Joe's lifeless hand and extinguished it in the congealing pool of blood on the ground.

"Reed, get on the radio to CQ and let them know about Busch."

"Roger, Doc."

"Finn, undo that body armor and lay down. I need to take a look at your rib and do something for that cut on your forehead."

Reed opened the door to the truck and grabbed the handset for the radio. "Cobra Seven One, this is Cobra One One. Over."

"One One this is Seven One. Go ahead, over."

"Hey, roger, the situation's report is as follows: enemy has broken contact, twelve enemy Kilo India Alpha, one friendly Kilo India Alpha, and one friendly walking wounded. How copy, over?"

"One One, that's a good copy. Any requests over?"

"Yeah, Seven One. We have two dead vehicles. We will need a few trucks from battalion out here to tow them back. Also requesting one medevac helicopter. Over."

"One One, I copy two trucks from battalion for the vehicles and one medevac helicopter. We will get a bird on its way as soon as possible. Over."

"Roger, Seven One, we will hold tight until we hear the bird. One One, out."

Sara epitomized everything that a girl should be in Joe's mind.

Her brown hair framed her face that bore a smile that could light up a room when she entered. He first met her when he dated one of Sara's friends, and he was still shocked at how she knocked him off his feet with her beauty. Sara's dark brown eyes dug trenches in his soul when he walked up with plans to ask her to go on a date. He remembered thinking how the odds were stacked against him. Still, he charged forward. He tried to remember exactly what happened next and drew a blank. He just remembered hearing the group of girls from the class below his own giggling after he left their presence. Joe smiled to himself when he realized again that he had a date that night with the nicest and prettiest girl in town.

He willed himself to focus on cutting and finishing the alfalfa. Thinking about the girl on his mind, Joe sat on the iron horse pulling the mechanized sickle around and around the hayfield

Mother Nature must have known about the date and what Joe was thinking while he toiled in the field. She worked her magic through the setting sun and the soft breeze blowing across the landscape. The sun that had beaten down on his shoulders dipped lower in the western sky. It would hide parts of itself behind the silhouettes of clouds accented in pinks, oranges, and yellows. The first stars yearned to shine under the eastern skyline as they patiently waited their turn to play matchmaker over the young couple later that evening. The field of fallen hay lay peacefully in the meadow slowly releasing their scents of the countryside to the breeze. Joe finished cutting the last stand of hay and made his way home and into the heart of the sweetest girl in the world on their first date that evening.

Joe pulled the tractor up to the diesel fuel tank and parked it where the black hose could reach the tank in front of the tractor. He shut the tractor off and climbed down from the operating platform. The gravel in the farmyard crunched beneath his boots. The sound from the vacuum pump in the barn where he milked the cows was accompanied by the twitters and chirps from the sparrows in the shade tree near the white farmhouse.

He reached to the top of the tank and pulled the nozzle from its holster, and, with his left hand, unscrewed the cap on the green tractor's fuel tank with his left hand. He filled the tractor's tank while thinking about his date with Sara later that night.

"Hi, I'm Joe. Is Sara ready?" he practiced aloud.

The conversation over, Reed cursed, dropped the handset, and turned back to see Doc examining Finn. Finn was sitting on the ground with his shirt open in the cover and shade of a shell of a destroyed vehicle. The bruising swelled into a softball-sized globe on his chest.

Greg knelt next to the body of his roommate and best friend, who lay on the stretcher. The pain in his heart filled his soul and being. The machinery of war claimed the life of his buddy that he met in basic training almost three years before. Greg relived the jokes and hard times they experienced together.

Their brotherhood began in basic training while they were on a foot march through the Oklahoma countryside near Fort Sill. After going to jump school together and reporting to the same unit at Fort Bragg, North Carolina, they shared the same room in the barracks. The memories of getting drunk and chasing girls with other buddies made them fast friends. They knew more about each other than their own families.

Greg knew that Uncle Sam would tell Joe's folks that he was killed in combat action somewhere in Baghdad. His love for his fallen brother and Joe's family compelled him to pull a note pad out of the breast pocket under his body armor and write a letter that Joe's folks would receive when Joe arrived home for the last time. Greg didn't know what to write, but he clicked his pen and began to pour his emotions and feelings out through the ballpoint pen.

He addressed it modestly to Joe's dad and then introduced himself. Greg told his brother's parents about how valiantly their son had fought to the end. He personified the fighting spirit and patriotism as best he could detail in his shaky hand-writing. A tear rolled down his cheek and fell onto the notepad and smeared a few letters. Sucking in his breath, Greg continued writing the letter.

He promised Doug and Sue to visit someday and pay respects to their family and Joe. He told them about how their son never lost his head and asked them how they raised such a selfless and modest man. He asked them not to think that their son's death was in vain because he fought to the end and how he died before he could reload and keep fighting.

Greg laid bare his own soul and was crying openly when he signed his name at the end of the letter. He picked up Joe's cold hand and held it to his chest and promised him that he would never forget their friendship. He promised to fight on to the end and to tell his children of the bravest man he ever knew. Greg opened the pocket on the right side of Joe's shirt and tucked the note inside.

"Hi, I'm Joe, Sara's date tonight." He said again.

He practiced his opening line and yearned to think of something smart to say without looking stupid when he met her parents before they left. He looked around to make sure that his younger sister wasn't spying on him while he practiced. He knew that if Kelli caught him, she would never stop her harassment. He rehearsed how to stand up straight but not too straight. He wanted to appear just the same as every other young guy without looking overconfident. He wasn't about to let a girl like Sara slip past him because he didn't make a good first impression on her parents.

The fuel hummed softly as it flowed through the thick rubber hose behind him. He practiced one more time. "Hi, I'm Joe." The hum turned into a gurgle when the tank was filled to the brim. He shut the fuel off, pulled the nozzle, and returned it to its holster. He practiced his walk with his shoulders back and head held high while he made his way back to the platform and fired up the tractor.

Exhaust plumed into the farmyard as he dropped the transmission into reverse and backed away from the tank. Pressing in the clutch, he put the machine in fourth gear and putted across the yard and into the red machine shed. He drove squarely between the giant sliding doors and into the darker interior of the building. Past the tool shop and oats bin, he parked the old girl in her normal spot against the wall. The distinct odor of burning diesel pleased Joe. His day of work was completed when he shut the tractor off for the last time that day.

He clambered down from the operating platform and slung his shirt over his sunburned shoulder and left the shed. The buzz of the vacuum pump his father used to milk the family's dairy herd grew louder as Joe stopped in the doorway and collected his thoughts. Contentedly drawing in a breath of fresh Iowa air, he smiled, and he took his first step toward the house to get ready for the big date.

He opened the screen door and stepped into a world filled with smells of fresh laundry and baking meat. His mother, Sue, sat at the kitchen table skinning potatoes for the family's meal that night. Fifty-two years young, Sue hid the gray in her hair beneath brunette hair dye. Her brown eyes sparkled in a round face with memories of raising a family in the countryside.

He walked into the washroom, and the screen door banged its way shut before Joe dropped his sweaty shirt into the laundry hamper and turned to the sink to wash his hands.

"Hey, Mom, how's supper coming?"

"Just peeling some taters. Are you sticking around for supper?"

"No, I have a date tonight. Dad let me out of doing chores so I could go," he said while he turned the knobs on the antique porcelain

sink and felt the water begin to flow over his calloused hands.   He picked up the slippery bar of Lava soap and started to build up a heavy lather.

"What's her name?"

He chuckled out loud, "Her name is Sara, Mom"

"Didn't you go out with a Stephanie Somebody last week?"

"Sure did," he answered as he dug the dirt out from under his nails.

"Must have a thing for girls that have names that begin with 's'."

"Sure do, Mom."

"You know you don't always have to be sarcastic."

"I'll learn my lesson sometime, I guess." He dipped his hands back under the running water and rinsed off the soap. "What are you making for supper? Smells like meatloaf."

"Good guess. We're having that with mashed potatoes and sweet corn."

"Remind me again why I'm taking a girl out to eat when I could have that here?"

"You could always bring her out here. I can hold supper if you want."

After shutting off the water, Joe picked up the hand towel off the rack on the wall next to the sink and dried his hands. "I don't want to scare her off on the first date."

"Well, sometime I'd like to meet one of these girls you're dating."

"I'll think about it. But now I have to hop in the shower or I'm going to be late."

Smiling to herself, she watched her son walk through the house. The potato in her hands made a shuck sound while she shaved off its skin. Slices of peel fell one after the other when Sue returned to making supper. Sue was unsure of her youngest son. She knew something was different about him, but she could not put her finger on what. Instead of dwelling on it, she returned to making the meal.

The medevac, which the survivors of the fire fight had ordered, hovered over the street taking orders from SGT Reed on the radio.

Finn sat up and leaned against the car before looking at Greg. "Hey, Sergeant, I'll keep an eye on him during the flight out of here."

Greg wiped his tears away, stood up, and walked over to Finn. "Thanks, man. Make sure you get that cut looked at too while you're at the hospital. I'll see you in a week or so when they send you back out here."

The blades of the chopper whipped the air and began to descend at the edge of the perimeter. The QRF pushed the perimeter to the end of the block as the medevac flared twenty feet off the ground. Dust and dirt cycloned around the men that shielded their eyes from the debris. Parker and Greg picked up the stretcher carrying Joe's body and began to run toward the helicopter while it set down on the cracked pavement. Doc pulled Finn to his feet and wrapped the soldier's arm around his shoulder and helped him to the open door.

Parker laid the front half of the stretcher holding Joe into the belly of the Blackhawk, and Greg slid the body of his best friend into the ride out of the combat zone. Finn climbed up and buckled himself into the webbed seat behind the pilots. Joe's arm had fallen off the stretcher and Greg reached out to hold his best friend's hand for the last time.

"I'll see you again, brother," he promised and laid the lifeless hand back on the stretcher and turned around.

After Greg moved away, SGT Reed gave the signal to lift off and take the men to the hospital. Greg blanched at the massive engines' whine and the blades' fight against gravity. The medevac lifted off and swung the tail around and streaked into the still-early morning sun. Greg picked up his rifle from the ground where he had left it to bring Joe to the chopper and dropped the magazine to the ground. He chambered another full magazine and picked the half spent magazine and placed it in his cargo pocket.

His body lying unconscious in the middle of a firefight, Joe soared in his memory through the air over his hometown, past the steeple of St. Boniface Catholic Church, over the welding shop and gas station. He followed his memory of driving in his 1991 maroon Buick Century sedan on an empty roadway traveling towards Dyersville. He cut off onto a dirt road just outside the town. He watched the all too familiar ranch house. He climbed out of the car. Joe's chest began to ache while he watched himself walk, his knees shaking, toward Sara's front door for their first date. He witnessed his love for Sara begin to blossom into the beautiful flower it would become.

Then he remembered being shot while telling his men to get out of danger half the world away.

His palms sweating, heart thumping in his chest, he shifted nervously from one foot to the other at the front door of the brown, brick, ranch house. His old car waited; its engine idling in the driveway. A chubby little black dog sprinted to the entryway window next to the front door. Joe, his hand trembling, withdrew his index finger from the doorbell button.

The sound of chimes excited Sara's family pet into a fury, and he started jumping up and down, yipping at Joe through the front glass. A woman of about 45, her brown hair cut short and wearing glasses smiled at Joe when she walked through the house to greet him. Joe pulled open the glass, storm door trimmed in white steel and smiled a crooked grin, hoping Sara's mom could not see his knees knocking.

"You must be Joe," she said, opening the front door. "Rascal, hush up! Don't mind him, Joe. He likes new people. Come in. Come on in. I'm Jane, Sara's mother. Sara needs a few minutes yet. You know how we girls are. Now come on in and relax and talk for a few minutes."

"Thanks, Mrs. Broshen."

"Just call me Jane," she said.

"I'm sorry, Jane." Joe smiled crookedly and tried to talk. "How are you doing tonight?" Joe stepped into the entry way and looked around the house. It was nicely decorated with pictures of family hanging on the walls. Threads of blues, greens, and reds speckled on a solid cream background carpet. Sara's father watched television with the newspaper lying next to him. Her father relaxed on a blue couch. A cherry-stained oak end table with a glass top guarded each couch end. A simple lamp with a vibrant shade lighted by a dim bulb, shone on the T.V. remote control lying by the lamps base. A black, jumbo recliner, an overflowing magazine rack standing next to it, invited anyone to the far side of the room for relaxation.

The entertainment center captured the focus of the room. A flat screen, 27-inch television was perched in the center chirping the evening news and the day's events to its audience who only half listened. A silver DVD player with a green liquid crystal display portrayed the time of 7:58 PM in glowing green digits. Potpourri filled out the rest of the entertainment center against the main wall of the house. The coffee table standing away from the couch wore a doily under three candles in the center of its stained finish. The chubby, little dog that so eagerly yipped at the him before accepting the stranger peacefully lay down in his spot under the coffee table and watched his people converse.

"Hey, Joe. I'm Pat, Sara's dad. How was your day?" Sara's father introduced himself after he got up to shake his daughter's suitor's hand. Pat looked as if life treated him well. He was built with a six foot frame and had a middle age belly around his middle. Pat's hair remained full and thick, but had prematurely turned grey. He wore an old pair of blue jeans with a simple brown t-shirt with a small stain that looked like it originated from a drop of ketchup.

"It's going well, Sir. I had a long day cutting hay. Got a little bit of sunburn on the shoulders," Joe answered grasping Pat's hand.

Joe gave him a strong and firm handshake while he hoped that Pat did not notice the sweat in Joe's palms. "How was your day?"

"Oh, you know. Another day, another dollar. Nothing really new or interesting to talk about. Anyway, let's get down to business. What are your intentions where my daughter is concerned this evening?"

"My...intentions? Uh, we're, uh, going to go to a movie and umm..." Joe stammered.

"What do you mean, 'umm'? You better not have any thoughts of other than holding her hand, and you better think long and hard about that before you do that."

"Y...y...yes sir."

Sara's mother, Jane, who had gone downstairs to check on her daughter, yelled up, "Pat, you leave that nice, young man alone. Don't be trying to scare him."

"Too late, Honey. I'm one step ahead of you on this one," Pat said and chuckled. "Relax, Joe, I'm just messing with you. This is Sara's first date, and I always said I would try to scare the guy off before he had a chance to leave the house with my baby girl."

Joe's knees were visibly shaking, and the sweat felt as if it were running from his palms as his heart was trying to find its rhythm after not beating for the better part of five seconds.

"Just be glad that Jane got to me about five minutes before you got here. I was pulling out my gun. I had every intention of sitting here cleaning the shotgun and pretending to load it when you walked in."

"Trust me, Sir. I am glad that Jane got to you first." Joe managed to crack a smile at his own joke.

"Daddy, what did you do to him?" Sara asked as entered the living room.

"Don't worry; I was just getting to know him."

Sara walked over to Jane and gave her a hug and said, "I'll see you later tonight, Mom. What time do I have to be home?"

Pat looked at Joe, "She has to be home by 12:30; any later than that and I might have the shotgun out."

Still nervous with an unbalanced heartbeat, Joe mustered "Y-y-yes, Sir, twelve-thirty it is."

"You two have fun tonight," Jane said.

Joe turned to open the front door and stepped aside to hold it for Sara. "We will, Mom!" she said and walked past Joe. He could smell her perfume and shampoo as she walked by him their first date.

"It was nice meeting both of you and thanks for not pulling a weapon on me, Pat. It means a lot, and I will have your daughter home by 12:30. Have a good evening," Joe said closing the door. The couple on their first date could hear her father laughing inside the house through the open windows.

His attention was drawn to Sara's stunning beauty while they walked to the car that was parked in her driveway. Sara's hair was pulled up into a ponytail that bounced as she walked, and she tucked her purse under her arm. The lime green tank top she wore had spaghetti straps that tried desperately to cover the black bra straps that ran up and over her slender and tanned shoulders. Sara's shirt fit her young curves perfectly as her date's eyes were drawn down her body to the striped belt that slipped through the loops on her shorts. Her belt tied the whole outfit together with its stripes of green, pink, and white. Her legs ran for miles under smooth, tanned skin down to her white sandals. She walked around the front of the car and Joe hurried to his side. He was the luckiest man ever.

They climbed into Joe's car and listened to the click of two seatbelts shutting and the car's transmission being shifted into drive. Before he drove away, Joe could feel Sara's eyes searching him from top to bottom, taking in her first impression. He turned and looked at her where he discovered the doorway to Sara's soul in her deep brown eyes. His heart felt as if it would leap out and jump through his throat with what he saw in the window to Sara's being.

He could see himself in her eyes and knew that she saw herself in his. Time stood still, and the world stopped turning for the couple in the car on the driveway. Both knew that the other had looked deeper than anyone had ever looked before. They knew and understood that they both were as nervous as the other.

Joe realized that on that night, he lived in the company of an angel. In that moment of baring his soul through his eyes, she had tamed the devil inside him with a single look of compassion, caring, nervousness, and anticipation.

Neither knew the road they had chosen to walk together in that split second of a moment on a hot, July evening during their first date. Neither knew that the path would be the most fulfilling and rewarding experience of their lives, and it began with Joe saying, "You have beautiful eyes." They drove away on their first evening together.

Greg marched up to the lead truck and picked the handset up off the seat, "Cobra Seven One, this is QRF, over."

"Go ahead, QRF."

"Roger, be advised the medevac has lifted off, and we will secure the area until battalion gets the trucks over here to clean up this street. How copy? Over."

"QRF, I copy you are driving on with the mission at hand."

"That's a good copy, Forrester out."

He had a mission to complete and a battle to fight. He turned his attention to focus on making sure that not another man would fall to an enemy's bullet during his watch.

Joe watched himself drive through his memory and disappear into a cloud of dust before pulling back onto the highway. Immediately, he felt being sucked into a vortex of light and wind stretching his mind into an arc of light and being dragged away from his most precious memory and being dropped into a hazy fog at the base of a flagpole where his mother stood crying in the distance. The phantom that planted the seedling stood up and started to turn around revealing itself to Joe, who stood by the flagstaff.

A noise startled him, the first noise Joe ever heard in his horrifying and startling vision. The flag was ripped away in the whistling of air that carried the message.

Sue looked her son straight in the eye. Joe learned that his previous interpretations of this vision were completely wrong as his mother's message rang through his mind. He knew his mother loved him with all her heart. What she said bore more importance than anything he had ever heard in his life or experienced in this blink of time outside his body and in an entirely foreign reality.

She spoke when the draping flag was ripped away completely, tearing pieces of Joe's body, flinging them into the wind. Before he was thrown into the land between realities, the words his mother spoke struck him with more force than any bullet could rip through his body.

"Come home, Joe," she whispered.

Then he heard something...silence.

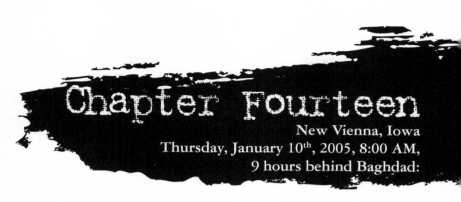

Chapter Fourteen

She stood in front of the kitchen sink in the old house that sat on 200 acres of rolling farmland. The goldfinches clothed in their dark winter feathers fluttered to and fro on the feeder outside the sink. Sue slowly washed the cookie sheets and moved slowly watching the nature show taking place only feet away above a snowdrift. The birds, oblivious to the human inside the house, spied on them as they feasted at the bird feeder.

The water in the sink slowly disappeared covered with suds that slowly disappeared while she caressed and washed the dishes. Sue couldn't wait for spring when the orchard outside was filled with apple blossoms and flower gardens that spread their buds in the spring and bloom into apples or various blossoms throughout the summer. The wind quivered and whispered through the sticks of trimmed stems in her rose garden. A draft seeped in around the window while she watched her husband of 30 years push snow onto small mountains throughout the farmyard.

The surreal scene brought Sue back to the memories of all her children growing up and playing outside. The coolness blowing through the window carried her back to a memory of her youngest son, Joe, running around in the backyard. He always loved playing soldier outside with his buddy being the family dog and performing make-believe assaults on the unsuspecting goldfinches and other random birds and wildlife. She knew he was a soldier at heart and a farm boy on the outside. Memories of Joe in cut off shorts, cowboy boots, and tanned skin was a pleasant relief from the constant worry that only a mother with her youngest son serving in a war knows and understands.

Joe's last letter home from Baghdad said that he was doing fine and that he missed her and the family. She knew that no matter what his letters said, Joe would never tell her anything about the war in Iraq that would worry her. Sue knew better than to believe everything she read because she could see the fear on her husband's face when he read his son's letters that were addressed only to him. A few weeks back she read one those letters she wasn't meant to read. Joe wrote to his father about the atrocities that he saw and the carnage taking place. Doug, his father, was the only person in the world outside the fighting that Joe would write to and tell the truth.

The sick feeling that came with reading about the close calls and bullets tearing past her son returned with the strength of morning sickness that only a mother knows. She never knew how Doug could read about that and not break into tears of worry and possible loss of their son. The stain from a tear that fell on that letter was still visible if she were to read it again.

That tear was filled with love and affection for Joe, her son who loved and cared so much for his country and family that he volunteered to serve with Army's famous 82nd Airborne Division. She tried to think why anyone would want to jump out of perfectly good airplanes, but then she remembered his telling her about the greatness of men that served before him in WWII. He said that these were the men that saved Europe and set the tough standards for being a paratrooper.

Sue pushed those thoughts from her mind and tried to think that another grandchild was going to be born in six months. Sue was ecstatic that she was going to be a grandma again. Joe and Sara's child would be her fifteenth grandchild. Secretly, she hoped that the child would be a boy to give Joe as many headaches and gray hairs as he had given and still gave Sue.

She still had a hard time believing that Sara told them before she had told her own family. They had made plans last night to share the wonderful news with her strict Catholic parents on the following Saturday. It was to be a women's day out at the spa where all three of them would relax in a sauna. Afterward, they would go out and splurge on a hot cup of expensive Cappuccino at the coffee shop.

The last thing Sara asked Doug and Sue was the quickest way for Joe to find out the fantastic news that he was going to be a father. Sue told her to contact the Red Cross with the news and then gave Sara his social security number to make sure that he would get the news as soon as possible.

Sue's brain took a violent turn out of left field when she began to think about Joe getting the news. It jerked her to a recurring nightmare that had been occurring since he deployed for this second tour. Her dream was a cloudy vision of Joe being home and never having to worry about a single thing ever again.

He was dressed in his dress greens bearing his full rack of awards shining with brass buttons and rank on his shoulders. His smile, which could warm anyone's heart and calm his crying nephews, was the part that troubled her the most. He stood on the front porch touching the service flag with the lone blue star, his pride of the sacrifice shining in his eyes.

In the dream, a strange car was parked outside with two people with featureless faces sitting in the front seats. She would reach out to hug her son when Joe would turn with a military sharpness and say to her, "You can stop worrying now because I am safe. I am home. Thank you for everything I never said I was thankful for. Tell Dad that I always looked up to him and loved you both from the depths of my heart. I love you both and will see you and our family again someday."

When Sue would reach out to hug him, Joe would turn and walk out the front door and salute the men in the car before walking to the flagpole and lowering the family flag. A tear from her son would fall on the flag when he hugged the colors and draped them over his shoulder. Her son would turn and mouth, "I love you, Mom," before walking down the dusty lane and disappearing into the afternoon sunlight glinting off the brass of his uniform.

Sue shook herself from the memory of the dream while the goldfinches were startled off the feeder by a strange car when it pulled slowly in front of the house with two faces hiding behind tinted windows in the front seats. Doug walked up from the machine shed to greet the strangers when they stepped out of the black Ford Taurus. The passenger was dressed in black with a single, white square on his neck. Doug and Sue recognized him as Father John from their church. The tall and clean-cut driver was wearing a uniform also and was the same as Joe's. Decked out with ribbons and brass and shined black boots, the soldier walked around the front of the automobile. Sue could not understand why Father John from church was with the soldier.

Father John broke the silence of the countryside dairy farm first. "Doug, Sue. I am so sorry."

The driver in the uniform was next. "Are you Mr. and Mrs. Busch?"

"Please, don't say what I think you are here to say..." Doug said quietly.

Father John reached out and took Sue's hand as Doug wrapped her in his arms and started to cry.

"Mrs. Busch, there is no easy way to say this..."

Chapter Fifteen

Baghdad, Iraq
Thursday, January 10th,2005, 0805 hours,
9 hours ahead of Dyersville, Iowa:

Dust flew throughout the battle site engulfing the men on the ground. It pelted their faces with dirt, soot, and glass. Spent brass shells rolled away into the gutters and clinked into the sewer. The burning Dodge Omni was extinguished for only a moment while the medevac lifted off. The car burst back into flames when the chopper was airborne.

Finn unhooked the seatbelt to allow the air medic to cut open his brown t-shirt and check his vitals while they cruised over the Tigris. Joe's bloody body armor lay spread open on the deck of the chopper, his collar flapping in the wind. His cold hand flopped to his side by an air current. His eyes fluttered open. Finn gasped while his pulse was being checked. He watched his dead Sergeant lie there on the deck, his toes pointing at weird angles into the wind whipping through the open doors.

Finn stared at the lifeless eyes that seemed focused on him. Joe's mouth slowly drooped when the muscles in his face relaxed. Finn began to feel an unstoppable sob rising in his throat.

"You okay, man?"

"Yeah, I just...just...I can't look at him."

"Fuck, we forgot to cover him up," the medic said. He dropped Finn's wrist from taking his pulse and reached under the seat to pull out a blanket to cover Joe's body.

Finn looked one more time at Joe only to see his chest rise and fall.

It rose back up, more noticeably, and a fresh spurt of blood seeped out of his armpit.

"Oh my fucking God! He's alive!" Finn screamed over the chop of the rotors.

"What did you just say?"

"HE'S ALIVE!"

"Cool it, man. You took a hell of a blow." The medic looked at Finn as he began to unfold the green, wool blanket.

Finn pointed his forefinger and rambled. "Fuck you! He ain't dead. I saw him breathe! He fucking looked at me."

The medevac chopper flared as it began its final descent onto the landing pad at the Combat Support Hospital.

The medic turned around on his knee and was about to drop the blanket over Joe's face.

"SGT BUSCH! IF YOU CAN HEAR ME," Finn shrieked, "IF YOU CAN HEAR ME, BLINK. BLINK, SERGEANT! BLINK, FUCKING BLINK, GODDAMN IT!"

The wheels of the chopper touched down and the waiting team of Army nurses and doctors rushed out under the whirling blades with a gurney as the air medic felt a warm spot seeping into the knee of his flight suit and stopped to dip his finger into it. His right index finger inside a latex glove came back up stained bright red while Joe's chest rose.

It happened.

"Holy shit," whispered the medic.

It happened again. Joe blinked, and a tear trailed through the dirt on his cheek.

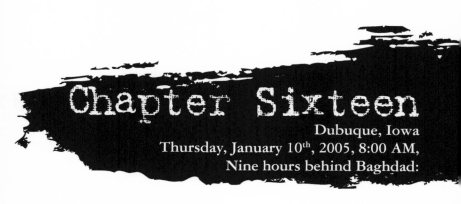

Chapter Sixteen

Dubuque, Iowa
Thursday, January 10th, 2005, 8:00 AM,
Nine hours behind Baghdad:

Piles of dirty snow lined the slushy streets of Dubuque, Iowa, and clung to the cuffs of Sara's jeans when she crossed the street to the offices of the Upper Mississippi Valley Red Cross. A box truck squished its tires through the salty and sandy muck that covered the street with potholes strewn about on Asbury Drive. Its exhaust tagged along floating above the ground like smoky streamers.

The biting wind clawed at her cheeks and tugged on the pink scarf wrapped around her neck. She pushed her hands farther into the parka jacket and clenched cold fingers around the movie stubs and ATM receipts she stuffed there. The icy handle on the outside of the frosted glass door tugged to her bare skin when she pulled it open quickly and stepped inside the small office. She felt the blast of warm air slap the chill out of her cheeks while she danced the snow and bitter cold from her jacket and out of her legs.

A warm face smiled at her from behind the receptionist's desk. The fiftyish woman with gray rooted hair spoke softly into the phone she held to ear. The receptionist covered the mouthpiece of the phone as she welcomed Sara. "I'll be right with you, Sweetheart. You can take a seat if you want."

"It's all right. Take your time," Sara said to the receptionist and turned around to read a bulletin on the cork board about the next blood drive.

The receptionist filled out the new appointment and hung up the phone. "Pretty chilly out there today, isn't it?"

Sara chuckled at the small talk. "Yeah, it is. It took forever to get my car to warm up on the way into town this morning."

The secretary stood and stepped out from behind the desk. "I bet. What can we do for you today?"

Sara unzipped her jacket and stuck her hands back into its pockets. "I have to send my boyfriend in the Army a message. I was told this was the fastest way."

"You heard right, Honey, but it depends on what the message is. I'm sorry to ask, but what do you have to tell him?"

Her face brightened with getting to tell a complete stranger her wonderful news, and her heart skipped a beat in her chest. "He needs to know that he is going to be a father, a daddy. Can you help me?"

"Oh my God, Sweetheart, that is wonderful news. Congratulations, how far along are you? You know you already have a glow about you." The giddiness of the secretary's voice infectiously spread throughout the small office, and the other ladies that worked in the Red Cross automatically knew and popped their heads over their computers and cubicles.

Sara smiled widely, "Three months."

The whole office, now aware of the situation up front, went up in a wave of awes and oooohs. They got up and acted like a bunch of school girls that just heard about one of their friends getting her first kiss and wanted to know all about it. They crowded around Sara. She answered all their questions, with an ever-widening smile and a warm feeling spreading through her chest.

Chapter Seventeen

Combat Support Hospital, Baghdad, Iraq
Thursday, January 10th, 2005, 0810 hours,
9 hours ahead of Dyersville, Iowa:

Nurses pushed the gurney up to the side of the medevac chopper. Their loose-fitting, green scrubs almost ripped off in the wash of the blades winding down just above their heads. A male nurse grabbed the foot of Joe's stretcher and pulled. The body board ground along the deck of the helicopter, rolling grains of sand through a mix of old and fresh blood.

"BP, 110 over 40. Pulse, 45! He was dead when we lifted off!" The air medic's words ripped from his lips into the wash of the main rotor still thumping in the air.

"Pulse is weak but there! Move it, people. Let's get him on the table. Moving on three. ONE! TWO! THREE!" yelled a male nurse with a stethoscope dangling from his neck. Joe's board slid onto the gurney that was nothing more than a fancy wheelbarrow. The medics pulled him out of the hurricane force winds and to the side of the landing pad.

Finn jumped out of the bird feeling the shock, of the hard asphalt beneath his feet bounce through his broken ribs. Hunched over with pain tearing through his side with every step, he tried to run a few steps to keep up with the body of his Sergeant. He stopped next to the gurney when they stopped to tighten the straps that held Joe on the green wheelbarrow.

The wounded soldier forced his way past a medic and picked up Joe's hand. "You're gonna make it, Sergeant! I'll be right here, man. Hang on!"

Joe's head rolled to the Finn's side as the hectic rush inside the hospital began. The chain of doctors, medics, and nurses kept a steady hand on the gurney or rushed ahead to open doors and prep the OR.

A light blinded Joe, and he squinted his eyes shut just when the train rolled through the doors.

Lights blinked one after another on the ceiling above the locomotive of life as conductors cut Joe's clothes off. "Specialist! You have to get out of the way! We have it from here." Someone ordered Finn to let go and step away. Joe's shredded clothes lay peeled off his chest and legs like a human banana. When the train stopped under the gigantic surgery light in the operating room, Joe opened his eyes. The lost look scattered when he fixed on the only man wearing a helmet.

Finn bent over trying to breathe through the pain and squeezed Joe's hand, "Sergeant?"

Joe sucked in a jerky and short breath, "Did we win?"

"Yeah, Sergeant, we got everyone out."

"Am I going to die?" Joe whispered.

The pain in his chest brought Finn to his knees, "You already tried that once."

"You need to take care of yourself, Finn."

"Need what?"

"You need to leave NOW, Specialist!" The same medic who ordered Finn on the pad to get away repeated the order when he started an IV in Joe's other arm.

"Fuck you!"

"Finn, get my mail. I'll make it," Joe gasped, and his eyes shut.

"He's crashing. Pulse is fading!"

Finn let his Sergeant's hand slip out of his grip and dropped backward to the floor. He crept toward the stainless-steel, cabinet-lined wall. Out of breath and energy, he sat alone and watched the feet of the men and women as they opened his Sergeant's chest.

"Get out of my sight!" Mrs. Busch shrieked. "Do not tell me my son is gone! Do not tell me that…" Sue yanked her hand from the priest's and fell into Doug's arms. She cried into his jacket, "Don't tell me that he won't be a father."

"Sue," Father John started to say. "Joe's not gone."

"What do you mean? What are you doing here?" Doug asked the Army Sergeant.

With his head bent against the winter wind, the soldier with Father John reached into the inside pocket of his overcoat and pulled out a folded, yellow paper. "We were notified early this morning that Sergeant Joseph Henry Busch was wounded in action around 0800 hours, January 10th, in Baghdad, which would have been around midnight here last night, the ninth. I'm sorry, Ma'am, if we gave you the impression that he was killed."

"You mean…are you saying…?"

"Yes, Ma'am, Sergeant Busch should be coming out of surgery soon, and as soon as he is stable, he will be transported to Germany and then back stateside. Your son is coming home."

"Is there any way to know if he will get the Red Cross message that he was being sent today?" Doug asked.

"We won't have any way to know that information, but you might be able to contact the Red Cross," The Army representative said. "If he is able to speak, he will be assisted in making a phone call home to you so the doctors can tell you what to expect. And we have the best field hospital in the world in Baghdad."

Sue's heart began to beat again after what had felt like an eternity of having her world collapse around her. She took a deep breath, consoling her fears over the horrible nightmare that Joe had been killed in Baghdad. Hardly a consolation thought that Joe had been wounded, "He is coming home though?"

"Yes, Ma'am, Joe *is* coming home."

"Nurse...Get that man out of my OR!"

A surgical nurse walked over to the collapsed Finn and squatted down on his good side. "Let's go. Your sergeant is in good hands." She took Finn's hand and pulled it over her shoulders.

Finn used the nurse to get to his feet and pushed against the cold, steel door behind his back. Together they walked out of the OR while a bone saw cut his Sergeant's chest open. Finn rested against her while she led him down the hall to the next room. After helping him onto the observation table, she adjusted the back of the bed to allow him to lean back and try to get comfortable.

She pulled a cart to her side to get a scissors and began cutting off his shirt. An ugly black and blue was mixed with a spreading pink through Finn's left side. He kept his head against the crunchy paper that covered the tiny pillow at the top of the bed. He gritted his teeth against the stabbing pain of his bottom two broken ribs grinding against each other. The nurse palpated the spreading bruise checking for internal bleeding and swelling.

"Your ribs are broken. They're in the right spot for healing, but I have to wrap the site, all right?"

"Aren't you going to go back to the other room? Don't they need you in there? I'm fine. The man in there needs more help than I do," Finn said gritting his teeth through the tears flowing down his cheeks and sides of his face.

"They won't miss me in there, and you need attention, too." She gently told him, "How about we get you sitting up so I can wrap your ribs." The nurse put an arm around Finn and softly started to bring him forward.

She pulled some gauze and tape from the cart and began to wrap his chest. Finn helped her with his good arm holding and handing her the tape and gauze or scissors when she needed one or the other. He sat, and she wrapped him in silence. Finn thought about Joe in the next room with his life in strangers' hands and thought about how he should have been able to see and shoot whoever got Busch.

The nurse heard his breathing quicken and shutter. When he missed his cue for the scissors and something landed on the nurse's hand, she took her purple gloves off. She reached up and grabbed his chin and turned Finn toward her. His cheeks were soaked, and the grown man sobbed gently. "There's nothing you could have done differently," she whispered and pulled him to her shoulder.

Finn let it all out. His muffled sobs came through the words. He apologized to the nurse for crying and apologized again and again for "fucking up." He cried into her shoulder while his tears stained her scrubs. "It should be me on that table. It should be me dying." He cried out, "Joe was yelling for everyone to get down when he caught the hot one."

"You're not responsible. Do you hear me?" she whispered and pulled him tighter. "You gotta do what you can to help him get through this. I know that he'd want you to get fixed up." Her brown hair spilled across his forehead as she held a man blaming himself for something over which he had had no control.

Combat Support Hospital Operating Room, 0840 Hours:
"Suction! Get this blood out."

Joe's ribs were spread wide under a blazing, white operating light. Bloody, surgical sheets covered his torso while the chief surgeon finished stitching the left branch of Joe's windpipe shut. Clotting blood pooled in the recesses of Joe's chest where his lung used to be.

A nurse carried a tray to the scale where a doctor weighed Joe's lung. It looked more like hamburger than the normal, grayish white. The pile of tissue's weight was spoken into a voice recorder and then replaced on the nurse's tray.

She turned around and started around the table. She held the tray at her waist, trying not to look at the destroyed lung. A crack in the floor seemed to shoot up and grab the toe of the cover on her shoe and held fast. The tray flew into the air. The pile of shredded lung shot off and hit the floor with a sickening splat while the nurse shrieked through her fall. She reached out to catch herself. Her left hand landed in Joe's lung on the floor, spreading it like a tough pile of Jell-O into her fingers before sliding out from under her hand to roll and slide across the tiles.

"Nurse! Pick that lung up!" the surgeon yelled. "And then get out of here and clean yourself up."

The young nurse crawled across the floor holding her tears back, picked the shredded lung up, and raised herself to her knees. The bullet and bone fragments pulled from the young soldier rested inches from her face when she put the meaty pile on the table.

The chief surgeon gave the order to finish suctioning as much blood as possible out of the man's chest and began prepping for closure.

"Chief, we got a problem..." Another nurse held the suction hose up in the air. "Take a look behind his heart."

The chief surgeon gently lifted the weakly beating heart exposing yet another glaring pearly shard of rib bone sticking up at a strange angle from Joe's spine. He reached in and said aloud to the crew around Joe's body, "We have no option, here."

He held the heart up with one hand and grasped the shard with his other hand. He pulled firmly and gently exposing fraction after fraction of more rib bone from Joe's spine when something caught. Before he could stop his arm, the chief surgeon ripped it free from the snag, and the final half inch was shaped like a fishing hook.

Chapter Twenty

New Vienna, Iowa
Thursday, January 10th, 2005, 4:30 PM,
9 hours behind Baghdad:

The men in the family gathered around the kitchen table inside the house they either grew up in or married into. The kitchen was quiet that night, words barely being choked out under the whispering of the ceiling fan. Rusty, Joe's dog, refused to get the cows into the cattle lot that afternoon. Instead, the dog chose to lie in his doghouse and watch the snowstorm build in the western sky.

Everyone in the family was called as soon as the priest and Army representative left in their ominous, black car. James, Joe's oldest brother and eldest in the family, arrived home first. He took off work for the rest of the day and week when he heard about Joe. Already aged from drinking and smoking, his weathered, sun-beaten face showed streaks and smears from wiping away tears. The words that Doug barely croaked out on the phone still rang in his ears.

"Jim, you have to come home. Something happened..."

"Hang on, Dad...what happened?"

"It's about Joe. A man from the Army came with Father John." Doug tried to tell him. "He was hurt in Iraq."

"How bad?"

"We don't know..."

James tried to push away the thought that kept creeping into his head. He forced himself to ask the impossible. "Dad, did they say if he would make it?"

He knew his kid brother would want to go quickly and painlessly if he had to go. James knew the truth though. There was no such thing as going quickly and painlessly in combat.

"They didn't say. You have to come home we need you and everybody here."

"Do you want me to call any of the others?"

"No, this is my job," Doug said. His voice broke before he hung up.

Jim was yanked out of his memory by the stinging taste of a teardrop on his lip. Once again he smudged the dirt and grease on his face when he proudly wiped away the tear, forcing himself not to cry anymore. He looked around and saw Daniel sitting with his hands clasped around Doug's at the end of the table where both men sat crying openly. Brian Cook, their brother-in-law, stood a few feet away with his back to the table, looking at a picture on the wall.

The volunteer fire-fighter, who had wormed his way into Nichole's heart and married into the country family four years ago, sucked back the pain and tears. He only knew Joe for a comparatively short time, but he knew the first time that he met the young man six years ago, when he was dating Joe's oldest sister Nichole, that Joe was born a different breed. He always silently envied and identified with the young man's light-heartedness and appreciation for life that only volunteers who put their lives on the line understand. Brian's big frame was brought low by the news that his second family had to go through and deal with something out of the ordinary.

When Daniel asked everyone to sit down and talk to "start getting some of 'this' off our chests," Brian sucked in a big breath and blinked twice before turning around to face the brothers and father that were bound by blood. He felt a need to maintain his composure, to be the rock that everyone could lean on and depend. Brian knew that his wife's family would need an outsider to be there and listen to the stories and memories of growing up and raising their kid brother who might not come home.

Brian turned around and walked to the corner of the countertops and leaned against the cabinets. He paused and pushed a picture of Joe during Christmas last year out of his mind before pulling out a chair and taking a seat next to Dan.

Dan, barely able to speak, looked across the table at his father and James sitting next each other. Jim, with his arm over his dad's shoulders, comforted the old man while silent tears fell unashamedly from his weather-beaten face.

Daniel was dealing with his own memories and emotions of knowing not only that another American soldier had fallen, maybe not to rise again, but also that this time it was Joe. This time it hit home.

Daniel was not distanced from the war as much as he thought. The war finally stretched from the deserts of the Middle East to a small town in the Midwest. The cold and uncaring machinery of war fed itself on the blood of his brother. It fed on the salty teardrops that dripped off grown men's cheeks.

Daniel knew what loss truly meant now. His heart was broken in a way that he thought would never happen. He wanted to turn back time to the last time he had seen Joe and shook his tough, soldier's hand. He wanted to share so many things about Joe but might not be able to now. He wanted to thank him one more time for fighting and tell him how proud he was of his younger brother volunteering to serve in the Army. He wanted to tell Joe that he was his hero and his definition of what a man should be. He wanted to learn from Joe. He wanted to learn how to live every day and appreciate every moment that life gave to them. Daniel did not want to learn these lessons in the way that their dear, old Uncle Sam was teaching them.

The feelings of pride from seeing the family flag waving gently in the winter wind were over-shadowed by the bare top half of the icy, white flag pole, only hours before the same flag was waving proudly at full mast. Feelings of sorrow came from knowing that their proud flag was flying at half-mast on the only pole in the county. Probably more, he thought, in the entire country. Salty tears dropped from his eyes when he broke the silence. "How's everyone holding up?"

"I don't know what to think, really," Doug replied. "I can't even really think."

"Yeah, it's so hard to even think about it. I never thought that this would happen," Brian told everyone at the table. "I mean, we all had to think this *might* happen, but we never thought that it really would. If that makes any sense...."

James couldn't help but smile and half chuckle. "Hey, you guys, remember a few deer seasons ago when Joe saw like thirty deer and unloaded his gun like three times? We were all up at the trucks waiting for him to come out of the timber when we heard one shot after another after another. We ran up over the ridge thinking that there would be a pile of deer lying around the tree line, and there wasn't a single dead deer. Do you guys remember how he just smiled and said, 'Damn...I must have missed a few.'"

"Yeah, he always had that dumb, little grin." Dan couldn't help but laugh, "You just knew that whatever he did or didn't do, he was going to be happy about it."

"'I must have missed a few.'"

Brian smiled to himself remembering that hunt, "We called him 'Trigger' after that one. He was the only one to see any deer, and he missed."

"He was crazy like that sometimes, wasn't he?" Doug said. "We don't know yet though, guys. We're still waiting on some news as to how Joe is. All we know is that he was wounded, and I've heard him say they have a pretty good hospital over there."

"Hey, Dad, you were in the Guard back in the day. I know Vietnam was going on then, and you know better than any of us what drives the guys in the service. Did Joe ever tell you why or how he did it?" Daniel asked their father. "Did he ever explain what drove him to be a paratrooper?"

Doug sat in silence and thought about the question. When Joe came home from basic training, the two had stayed up talking at the kitchen table one night. They swapped stories and chided each other like two old buddies. Doug remembered that he saw a shadow of himself sitting across the table that night. He remembered hearing his young soldier telling about basic training, the drill sergeants, and his first jump at jump school. Doug decided then to let his sons who surrounded him know about a secret that only service members know.

"It's not something very complex," he said. "It's the same thing that drives you and me every day, but to a whole new degree, I think. He never did it because he wanted to think he was better than anyone else. I think he did it simply because he wanted to serve. I think he wanted to fight and defend all of us. If I had to put a reason behind why Joe and those paratroopers do it, it would be because they don't want anyone else to do it. They know what they're getting into and would rather have it be them who fight and die than someone they know and love. I know Joe did it because he didn't want to see any of us risking our lives. You know what?" Doug paused, "Hold on a minute guys, I'll be right back."

Doug remembered the last package he got from Joe and what was inside. Joe knew something was about to happen to him or his unit, and he included some of his writings from being bored over there. Doug remembered that after reading all of it, he thought Joe had turned into a decent writer somewhere along the lines.

Joe included in his last package a note about how badly things were going in the war. He spent some of his free time putting his thoughts on paper. He included stories about deer hunting and an explanation about why he served. Doug remembered feeling pride in his son the way he'd never felt. He was able to identify and, for a fleeting moment, knew the complete reasons behind Joe's sacrifice.

Doug walked down the back hallway of the house, past the parlor where the girls in the family comforted Sue, and into the living room where a picture of Joe hung. It was taken about a year before when Joe was still only a specialist. He wore his dress uniform with the best maroon beret. The awards and decorations adorned his chest in rows of ribbons underneath the brilliant jump wings Joe had earned every time he jumped from an airplane. His marksmanship medal hung on the left side of his chest under the ribbons, wings, and French forge that laced under and around his shoulder. His face was missing a smile but showed the gravel in his gut and spit in his eye from endless training and discipline.

Doug sucked in a proud breath and took a left into the laundry room. He walked past the white Maytag washer and dryer and into his office. Doug located a brown envelope buried under a mountain of bills and paperwork on the desk. In it was Joe's explanation of why he fought and defended his family against an enemy even his trained eye couldn't identify.

Doug pulled it out from under the pile and watched bills flutter to the ground and land at his feet. His fingers instinctively opened the brass clasp and folded the flap over the top. Reaching in, he pulled out Joe's last letter home. Doug flipped past the first letter of his youngest son's handwriting and last will that Joe included with the letter, which he entitled "Dear

Ms. Liberty." Doug separated these and laid the rest of the contents on top of the envelope with countless post marks and stamps on the edge of the paperwork covered desk.

Doug rolled the letter up and retraced his same footsteps through the house. He no longer felt the urge to cry over his son's sacrifice as he approached the kitchen table. He walked over to the table on legs that felt younger than they had been thirty years ago and sat down.

"Here it is. This is from the last letters home that Joe sent." He told everyone around the kitchen table, "A week ago, he sent me a letter with his will and some writing that he wrote in his downtime over there. I read this, and I knew why he did what he did." Doug held the letter up and began to read it aloud.

"Dear Ms. Liberty,

I know in these troubled times that standing tall in your harbor welcoming the nameless from foreign shores while holding your torch high is tough. I am writing this letter to you tonight to ask you to stay strong and remind you that America's greatest generation is coming of age right now. We live in a horrible world filled with crime, corruption, and darkness. Our leaders have failed the people, and yet you have stood tall and shined brightly throughout it all.

My name is Joe Busch, and I hail from a small town in the heartland. I don't believe we have ever formally met before, but I consider you to be the greatest and most important figure in my life. You may have heard my name mentioned in foreign deserts and towns. Does SGT Busch of the United States Army ring a bell? I volunteered several years ago to serve in your defense and that of our great nation. While in your service, I was asked to carry a ray of light from your torch of freedom to Baghdad and dutifully spread your word and light to the streets of that foreign country. I showed what freedom meant to young children and old men in different cultures, who spoke varying languages, by my example in the uniform I wore. For my entire life, I have always felt the warmth and security offered by your flowing robe wrapped around me. With the knowing conviction that I will offer my own life for the continuance of your freedom light to remain burning brightly, I write to you today. Please keep standing tall in the face of everything that this cruel world wants to dump at our feet and blame on America.

Some people say that the greatest generation lived 60 years ago and who are dying off every day. I am telling you that the greatest generation to ever live is coming of age right now. We are a proud generation following the examples set by our grandparents and learning from mistakes made by our parents.

We are a generation that is more educated than you have ever seen, and I promise that medical discoveries will be made in the near future that will leave imprints deeper than those of penicillin and vaccinations. We will make footprints in the path of peace and unity where many thought it would never be possible to traverse. We will pave new roads in conservation because we see the end of our dependency on oil and irreplaceable fossil fuels.

We feel the sting and pain of the loss of the innocence we never knew. My generation was forced to mature at an earlier age because of the internet, and too many of us are raised in single parent homes... We see the lasting effects of these and are already changing to adapt and overcome so our children and coming generations might not know these. Yes, some of us still make mistakes, and blessings happen, but we promise to work hard for these children and promise to give them a better world than the one we were handed.

In our history, only one prior generation experienced a war lasting more than four years. Our fathers and uncles still tell stories of coming home to a nation unsympathetic to their sacrifices. They called our fathers' fallen brothers murderers, rapists, and baby killers. A part of their souls joined the souls of the 58,000 who fell in the jungles and highlands when they experienced that. I believe that part of the collective spirit of our nation died then, too. Today's generation is not like that. We welcome our soldiers home with open arms and warm hearts. We congratulate them for spreading your message, even if some of us believe that this war is unjust and wrong.

Earlier tonight, my nephew arrived into this world. His name is Cody Christopher Cook. Although I have not seen him yet, already I believe in him. I believe in his generation, but yet I worry. What is this world coming to? I look around and see unrest and turmoil abroad and at home. Our leaders cannot seem to come together for the common good. They forget the masses that they represent until it is election time. By then, it is too late, and they resort to dirty campaigns with never anything positive to say. They depend on belittling and derogatory remarks about their competition and in the end only confuse us, the people. I see this and cannot help but feel the threat to the liberty and freedom we hold so dear to our hearts.

Even though I believe with my entire heart and being, I wonder to myself, will Cody Christopher Cook ever truly know the warmth and security of the folds of your robe? Will he ever nurse from your breast to grow strong, fearless, and bold on your milk? Will my nephew mature through fear of terrorism, or will he mature through a time of peace and prosperity? Will my sister's child grow up in a peaceful time and walk the paths lit by your flame? I hope, with my soul on the line, that he will.

Some people have asked me in the past, "Why do you serve, Joe?"

My answer never changes. I serve you and our nation because I believe. I believe in myself, my generation, and my nephew. I believe in the memories of basking in the glow of your fiery torch. I believe in the strength of you and me standing strong against the world even if we are forced to stand alone. I know that these are trying times, and I want you to know that you, Ms. Liberty, are not alone. My generation believes you will not let us down. I give you my word and if necessary, my life, that my generation will stand with you and fight for the cause of liberty and righteousness because we believe.

I write to you tonight on behalf of my generation, the generation just arriving, and generations to come. I write to convince you to believe in us. For as long as a single person believes in your flame, it will continue to burn. As long as a single person believes in America as the Promised Land, America will clothe herself in your robe, light her way with your light, nurse from your breast to grow strong and bold, and warm herself in your arms. As long as one of us believes in you, I ask that you believe in us.

Ms. Liberty, I believe.

Sincerely,

SGT Joseph Henry Busch"

Doug looked at the men sitting next to him around the kitchen table. Not a single tear was visible. Doug never thought that a man could actually see pride and patriotism until that moment. The amount of pride that everyone felt in the possible forfeiture of their brother's and his son's life was unimaginable. Brian fought back a tear because the child Joe wrote about belonged to him. Cody was born on November 13th, 2004, almost a month after Joe deployed. Brian never knew that Joe was so proud of being able to fight for the chance that Cody would have a peaceful life while he grew up.

No time remained for Doug to stay and talk because his dairy herd needed to be milked. Work needed to be done, and this gave Doug some time to think to himself and remember Joe in his own personal way, and he could start to plan how to tell Sara that her baby's father might not be coming home.

The nurse had gathered the scissors, tapes, and bandages together and put them back on the cart before she left the room to allow Finn some time to rest and compose himself. The young man felt embarrassed that he cried so openly in front of the pretty, brunette nurse. He had allowed a complete stranger to see his weak side, a side that every soldier has but never lets anyone see.

Finn wiped his face with the back of his arm and took a deep breath when he remembered his Sergeant's last order. His Sergeant wanted his mail, and Finn would be damned if he didn't have it when Joe came out of surgery.

Finn scooted off the edge of the table and crept toward the door of his room. His mind had already switched from painfully wounded back to soldier on a mission. The brunette nurse that wound his chest and set his ribs was disappearing around a corner in the hallway leaving the corridor completely vacant minus a cart full of blue scrubs that sat across the hall. Still without a shirt and with dusty combat pants on, Finn crept into the hallway and grabbed a scrub top and stole back to the room. He shook the shirt open and threw it over his head, almost passing out when he raised the arm on his bad side through the sleeve. He went over to the sink in the room and splashed some water on his face to clean the dust and grime off his shadow of a beard.

He had been in this hospital before and knew how to get to the communications room. Finn, dressed as a male nurse who couldn't use his left arm, walked back into the hall and started toward the "commo room." He did not know what he'd say when he got there, but he would get word to his unit, one way or another, that Joe was alive and needed his mail.

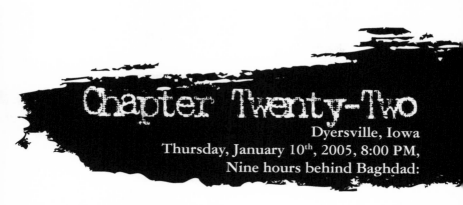

Doug finished chores early that night. Even the cows seemed to know that something extraordinary had happened. They allowed themselves to be milked without shifting in their stalls or swishing Doug with their tails. He shut off the local radio station's newscast informing the rolling countryside buried under a white blanket that the war machine had numbered "one of our own sons." Even though none of the broadcasts mentioned Joe's name, Doug's cell phone had begun to ring off his belt with people wondering if it was Joe who had been wounded.

He had driven his wife's minivan to a house in the countryside on the outskirts of Dyersville. The white Chrysler's tires crunched over the ice-packed road between mountains of plowed snow that lined the sides of the gravel road. The snowy tunnel reminded him of days gone by, days he hadn't known since years before Joe had been born.

He and Sue had talked on the way to Broshens about how they wished they could take their house phone, the landline, off the hook when they got back home. They had to tell Sara about Joe first. Still it was vital the family needed to be able to answer Joe's phone call, if he could or would be able to call.

The van's headlights lit up a frosty, midwinter scene in the Broshen yard. A deep pile of snow lay on their front lawn. Icy sidewalks and tree branches were lined with a coating of frost, and icicles hung from the corners of the gutters on the roof.

Warmth and light spilled out from the first floor windows, and a small lamp outlined a bedroom. Once Doug pulled in front of the Broshen garage, he reached over and intertwined his fingers with Sue's. Sue spent the short drive from home staring out the window, barely speaking.

"We have to be strong, Sue."

"I don't know if I can do this. She's expecting our grandchild." Sue started to cry and kept staring into the cold, winter night.

"We have to do this for Joe. It's what he would want." Doug squeezed her hand. "We have to be strong- strong for Joe."

"Don't let go of my hand, please?" She turned and spoke showing tear-swollen eyes. "Don't let go, Doug."

"I will never let go, Sue."

Doug shut off the van, got out, and went around to open his wife's door. He kept one hand in his coat pocket around the official, yellow paper from the Army that held the news. Doug wrapped his arm around Sue and held her steady while they walked up the icy sidewalk. The freezing night was completely still and clear. The stars shone brightly through frost covered branches reflecting off the snow making the world seem as though everything was at peace and dared anyone or anything to upset the balance.

They waited after ringing the door bell while Sara's little, black mutt ran up and started yapping at the window next to the door. Jane came shuffling through the house, trying to squint out into the darkness and see who stood at the door. She flipped the light on just above the door on the outside above Doug and Sue's heads. Immediately recognizing and getting more excited by the heartbeat, she tried to hurry even more to get the guests in from the bitterly cold night.

The door swung open, and little bells bounced inside the seasonal wreath on the door when Doug and Sue stepped onto the welcome rug and stomped the ice and snow from their feet. Options on how to tell the Broshens raced through Doug's mind while he held his wife in one arm and the yellow, official paper in his left hand.

"How are you folks doing tonight? It's been such a long time since we seen each other. What brings you out to this neck of the woods?" Jane prattled on like a little school girl giggly with an unexpected gift.

"Who's here, Jane?" Pat called from the kitchen.

"It's the Busches. Come and say hi and quit being lazy in there." Jane, still startled with her unexpected guests, said, "Where are my manners? Can I take your coats, or won't you be staying long?"

"I don't know how to say this, Jane," Doug began. "We heard about Joe today, and we need to tell Sara."

Jane paused for a split second, and she noticed the expressions the Busches wore were not from the cold, but rather from news that shatters a person's world. "Oh my...is it bad?"

"Come, Sue. Let's get out of these jackets." He released Sue from of his comforting half hug. "We should probably sit down to tell you and Sara. Is she around?"

"Mom, who's here?" Sara asked from down the hallway.

"Honey, ummm." Jane tried to calm her shaking voice. "Could you come down here for a bit? Joe's Mom and Dad are here." Jane took Doug's and Sue's coats and laid them over her arm. "Let's go into the kitchen and talk," she said guiding Joe's parents and laid their coats over the back of a tan, overstuffed recliner.

As Doug and Sue took a seat around the Broshen's antique oak table, Sara appeared in the doorway between the living room and kitchen looking apprehensive and worried. She bit her bottom lip and crossed her arms across her belly, subconsciously hoping that Joe's parents didn't show up at this time of the evening just to help her tell her parents about the miracle growing inside.

"Sara, I think you should sit down for this," Doug said.

She was worried now. She had never seen the Busch's expressions on anyone before, not even when she told them about her being pregnant. She unwrapped one of her arms from around her and shuffled her slippered feet across the floor and pulled out the chair between Jane and Sue. "What's wrong, Sue?" she asked sitting down and pulled one leg up to hug and rest her chin.

Sue reached out and latched onto Doug's hand as though admitting the news would make the horrible reality even truer. Sue looked deeply into Doug's eyes for some strength, anything to help make all the pain disappear from her heart. Sara put her hand on Sue's back when she saw the tears begin to flood Sue's eyes. That's when the Broshen's attention was drawn across the table to a yellow piece of paper that Doug began to unfold with one hand on top of the table.

"What is that?" Sara took a deep breath, as if not wanting an answer. "Is that...? Don't tell me that that is what I think it is..." Her voice began to break into thousands of shards which her heart had splintered into.

"Sara, before I read this, have you told your mom and dad what you told us last night?"

Sara, unable to speak, laid her head on her knee as she crumbled like a house made of coffee grounds. She muffled her sobs through biting her knee and let the tears run down her cheeks. She tried to speak, but nothing came out other than muffled moans yelled into her pajama pants-covered knee. She hugged her leg even tighter, trying to squeeze the pain of shame from her soul, the pain of not knowing what that damned, yellow piece of paper was.

Sue leaned over to her and wrapped her up in a hug while she looked at Jane sitting there with her puzzled, worried, and bewildered look. Sue buried her face in Sara's shoulder and cried with her. Sue told her everything would be okay and asked if she wanted her to tell her parents. Sara let go of her leg and wrapped Sue in a tight hug before letting go. She shakily nodded.

Sara let Sue out of the hug and swiveled around in her chair to face her parents. She put out her hands and hoped that her mom and dad would put their hands in hers. "Mom, Dad..." She paused to look around the table, "I'm going to have a baby. Joe is the father."

Chapter Twenty-Three

Recovery Room, Combat Support Hospital, Baghdad, Iraq
Thursday, January 10th, 2005, 1630 hours,
9 hours ahead of Dyersville, IA:

"Stop that man!"

Finn ran as hard as he could through the hospital corridor with every breath feeling like a knife was being driven between his broken ribs and twisted when he breathed. Finn threw carts and trays into the path of the soldiers. The footsteps behind him grew closer and louder as the two pursuers jumped over the obstacles.

Out of nowhere, an arm swung out of an observation room clothes-lining Finn in the ribs. The young infantryman, who was visiting a wounded buddy at the hospital, climbed on top of Finn and rolled him facedown in the middle of the hall-way. He swung hard at the base of Finn's skull with the heel of his right hand, sending a blinding light through Finn's vision, temporarily paralyzing the specialist. He reached into the cargo pocket of his pants and pulled out a pair of white, plastic zip ties. With Finn unable to resist and barely able to breathe, the soldier swung both of Finn's hands behind his back and used the zip ties to handcuff the specialist, fully restraining him.

"Whoa! Easy there, killer. That man's on our side, and he has a few broken ribs. Get off of him," the taller of Finn's pursuers ordered.

"What the fuck? Why the fuck was he running like a mad man through the hospital?"

The second of the chasers, breathing deeply trying to catch his breath, responded, "He tried...tried to break into the commo room."

A crowd was beginning to form in the hall trying to get a look at the big man on the floor wearing a scrub top. "Well, he did break into the commo room. We caught him trying to mess with the radio to get in touch with his unit," said the tall one. "He saw us coming and leveled both of us as he tried to get away."

A full bird colonel stepped out of another observation room down the hall. "Get that man off the floor! I just got done sewing up his sergeant. All he fucking wanted to do was his sergeant's last order." He turned to the two who had pursued Finn. "Get him out of those zip ties, let him sit next to his sergeant and wait for him to wake up, and someone get word to this man's unit that their Sergeant is not dead!"

"Roger that, Sir." The guards said almost in unison and started forward to pick Finn up from the floor.

"Do it now! It doesn't take two of you to pick him up and bring him to his Sergeant." The Colonel turned and mumbled, "Fucking privates." He walked away from the chaos in the hallway.

Finn pulled himself to his knees. Being pissed off that he was tackled and tied up like a piss-ant Iraqi helped him block out his pain. "Cut these fucking ties off, you piece of shit guards!" His head still ached from the almost knockout punch by the grunt. "Nice moves, Private," he said to the visiting grunt with the common respect shown between two men who knew the streets of the deadly city.

As the shorter guard cut the ties off his wrists, Finn con-templated what to do next. He was unable to reach his unit because he didn't have enough time to set the hospital radios to match the encrypted frequencies that his unit used. He turned around while his guard tried to guide him to SGT Busch's room and hollered down the hall, "Tell them to bring his fucking mail. That's all he wanted...his fucking mail. You hear me?"

He looked down at the borderline midget guard and stared him in the eye. "You wouldn't last a day in our unit, much less on the streets of this city."

"Here's your Sergeant's room. Nurse, can you update this Specialist on the status of his Sergeant?" he said to the same nurse who had bandaged Finn's ribs. "I'll be outside this doorway. You're not to leave this room until your unit comes for you. Do you understand?"

"Yeah, I fucking understand that." Finn rubbed his wrists as he walked to his Sergeant's side and stood next to the pretty, brunette nurse who had comforted him earlier.

"One last thing, Specialist," the short private looked at him from the doorway. "I've been on the streets. That's why I'm in here. It's a lot tougher watching men come in here to die after doing everything you can to help them than it is killing hajji out there."

The nurse put her hand on top of Finn's to calm him and whispered, "He's like that all the time. Just let it go. Let it go." She adjusted an IV in Joe's arm and checked the drip. "The best thing we can do now is to talk so Joe can hear us when he starts to come out of this."

Finn pulled his arm away from the touch of the nurse, and started walking away but stopped just shy of the door. He thought for a second and opened it.

"Finn," the nurse pleaded when she heard the shoving and a loud crash in the hall.

"He didn't deserve to have a seat out there," Finn said. A smile crossed his face when he offered the chair stolen from the guard in the hall to the pretty, brunette nurse. "But, you do."

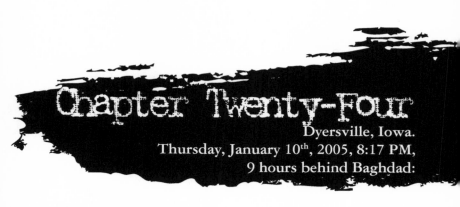

Chapter Twenty-Four

Dyersville, Iowa.
Thursday, January 10th, 2005, 8:17 PM,
9 hours behind Baghdad:

"Oh my God! Sara!" Jane cried totally shocked and surprised. "Come here," she pleaded as all three women began to cry.

"I...I didn't know how...how to tell you. I didn't... want... to disappoint you. You've always been there...for... me." Sara sobbed inside the bear hug of her own and Joe's mother.

"Sara, Baby Doll!" Her dad got up from his chair and took a knee beside Jane's chair and put his hand on her knee. "This is the most wonderful thing. I know we haven't told you as much as we should have, but we love you, no matter what."

The group of women pulled together even tighter, depending on one another to survive the news. Whispers through tears floated out for Doug and Pat to hear promises for help to get Sara through this, "no matter what happens."

Sue cried harder and different tears than the Broshen women when she broke the hug and looked to Doug across the table. She reached out her hand, and he folded his hand around hers and squeezed.

"Doug," Pat asked, "what's the real reason you came over tonight? I can tell by the look on your face that you have some other news, and you're holding a piece of paper that looks... official."

Sue squeezed Doug's hand back before letting go. She put her index finger under Sara's chin and pulled Sara to look at her. "Darling, did you get to the Red Cross today?"

Sara attempted to wipe her eyes dry with the sleeves of the oversized Army t-shirt she wore. "Uh-huh. I sent the message this morning."

"Because what we found out today will be even tougher to tell you now." Sue did her best to control her emotions.

"What news? What did you hear? Is he all right? What happened to Joe?" She pushed herself back from the table out of her mother's arms and she tried to read Doug and Sue's faces. Her heart collapsed even more into itself when she saw the yellow paper she had momentarily forgot about when she told her parents that they were going to be grandparents.

"Doug...don't tell me!" she begged, and she stood backing against the wall behind her. "I need him. I can't do this alone!"

The two mothers got up to go to her side, but she only pushed them away. "Tell me, I need to know he's all right..." she cried loudly.

"Sara," Doug began, barely able to keep his voice from breaking. "Joe was hurt today. He was hurt pretty bad."

"NO!" Sara moaned. "He can't be. He promised me he'd come home." Sara slid down the wall to the floor. "He doesn't know he's going to be a daddy. He doesn't know how much...I never told him how much..." Sara's breaths came and went in shallow gulps, barely able to keep her from fainting. She shook her head side to side, futilely trying to push the words from her mind. Sara clawed at the black letters on Joe's t-shirt she wore to bed every night. She tried to scratch the Army out of her life and off her chest and slapped away the helping hands of her own and Joe's mother.

"Jo-o-e," she wailed and wept bitterly.

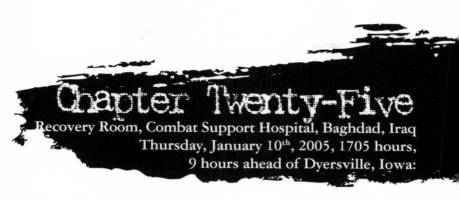

Chapter Twenty-Five

Recovery Room, Combat Support Hospital, Baghdad, Iraq
Thursday, January 10th, 2005, 1705 hours,
9 hours ahead of Dyersville, Iowa:

Finn sat down on the foot of SGT Joe Busch's bed, and the pretty, brunette nurse took the chair that Finn stole from the guard in the hall. They started talking about anything and everything they could.

Finn told stories of growing up in Iowa and how he and Joe formed a special bond just knowing a lot about each other and the small-town lifestyle they had experienced. Finn discovered that her name was Audrey Marie Clariski. Audrey Marie Clariski, from St. Paul, Minnesota, graduated with the class of 2000 of the University of Minnesota with a Bachelor's of Nursing Science Degree. She had two younger brothers, both of whom served in the Minnesota Army National Guard.

Audrey seemed to close up when Finn asked if they had done any tours overseas. A simple yes was all she said before quickly asking Finn about his hometown. They kept talking small talk for a while about Finn's hometown of Storm Lake, Iowa, until he asked Audrey why she volunteered to be a nurse in a combat hospital.

She turned away, and her voice choked up a bit. Finn slid from the bed and took a knee next to her and put his good arm over her shoulders. "I'm sorry. It wasn't my place to ask that sort of question, Audrey."

She put a hand over his and sniffled. "No, it's just really personal, Alan." Audrey squeezed his hand and began again,

"They both served over here in the beginning. Jeff and Sam served in the same unit together."

"Audrey, you don't have to tell me this, if you don't want," Finn said when she paused to blink back the flood springing from her deep hazel, almost grayish-green eyes.

"No, I started, and it's time I start facing the facts that no matter what I do, they won't be coming back."

"I'm sorry," Finn said and pulled her closer with his good arm. "I'm here. I won't go anywhere."

"They were together on a patrol when they got ambushed by an Iraqi Army patrol. Jeff saw the grenade being tossed. He and Sam were lying there together returning fire when that grenade rolled between them. Sam pushed Jeff backward and picked the grenade up to toss it over the mound they were lying behind." Audrey stopped for a deep breath and wiped a teary streak from her face. "It blew up when he released it. He died in Jeff's arms." Audrey couldn't go on and turned to cry on Finn's stolen, blue scrub top.

"It's okay, Audrey. It's okay," Finn whispered. "There's nothing you can do now to bring him back."

"That's not it though." She pushed herself away from Finn's shoulder to look him in the eye. "When Jeff got home, he wouldn't stop blaming himself for Sam's death. He kept waking up in the night screaming Sam's name in nightmares. He was afraid to go to sleep, to eat, to drive. I tried to get him to a counselor for PTSD, but the guard wouldn't let him go." Audrey trembled. "It got so bad that at the end...he...he...took his own life."

"Oh, Audrey, I'm very sorry. I had no idea." Finn cupped the back of her head while she laid it back on his shoulder and wept.

Her words muffled by sobs of talking about her brothers' dying, Audrey unloaded the baggage she had been carrying all along. "It's okay, Audrey. I'm here for you. Let it out." Finn kept whispering into her ponytail while she wept.

"That's...that's... why I...I volunteered," she sobbed into his shoulder. "I want to do what I can to make sure that never happens again."

They stayed like that until a moan from the bed behind them roused them from their bonding. Audrey raised her head and looked at Finn with amazing depth and understanding in her eyes.

"Is Sergeant Busch waking up?" Finn asked.

"I think so," Audrey said softly.

Finn spun around on his knee and looked at his Sergeant lying on the bed. Joe lay motionless, covered in bandages with tubes sticking out of every possible natural and some new orifices. "Sergeant, are you there?" he asked loud enough to wake the man in the next room. The specialist got up from his knee and walked softly to the bedside, across from Audrey who was checking Joe's vitals. Finn wrapped his hand around Joe's, leaned over, and said, "Sergeant, if you can hear me, squeeze my hand twice."

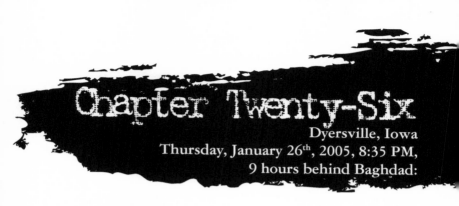

Sara sat on the hardwood floor with Jane's and Sue's arms around her shoulders. Doug and Pat knelt on both sides, holding her hands. She cried herself dry of tears and struggled to gain control of her breathing. Several times she tried to say something, anything, but the words that Joe was wounded and that no one knew anything more, kept ringing through her head. Her heart kept shattering into tiny sharp shreds of muscle that felt as if it couldn't go on beating any longer.

She felt as if she were going to throw up, always swallowing the empty clump back down her throat and into the empty pit of her stomach. Sara let go of Doug's and Pat's hands and wrapped her arms around her belly trying to protect her baby from the horrible news. She hoped and prayed the tiny, helpless baby would never know how dreadfully alone she felt at that moment. Her entire world had been torn away from her grasp. Her soul searched for someplace to lie itself down and cry itself to sleep.

Sara had plans that she never told anyone about–plans that she had started to lay out on her mind's drafting table before she found out she was carrying a baby. She decided even then that she wanted to spend the rest of her life with Joe. No matter what happened over there. She wanted to help him get used to civilian life after he got out of the service. She wanted to be there to rub his back when he woke up in the middle of the night with nightmares that he was sure to experience. She wanted him to be her man, her husband, her partner in life.

The pain filled her chest, and she began to cry fresh tears. Her mother's words mixed with her cries for God to let Joe come home.

Sara wanted to run out into the freezing winter weather and fall naked into an icy snow bank or dip her feet into boiling water, anything to take her mind off the dagger that split her chest beneath her left breast. She searched the faces around her in the kitchen for answers. Anything that would end her pain. She fainted looking for answers that weren't anywhere to be found that night.

Audrey and Finn waited at Joe's bedside for any sign that he was conscious-a blink of an eye, a hand squeeze. They stood there, silent, oblivious to the footsteps of hospital personnel going back and forth in the hallway. The only noise in the room was the rhythmic beeps from the EKG machine and the rising and falling rustling of the respirator pushing fresh air into Joe's only lung.

Audrey left to get a warm washcloth and clean some of the blood that had started to ooze from under Joe's bandaged armpit. She returned and started to sponge the skin around the saturated wrapping. Finn's spirit grew hopeful when the EKG machine's beeps slowed momentarily, then started picking up in tempo. "SGT Busch! Squeeze my hand if you can hear me!" Finn said excitedly.

His loud order caused some footsteps in the hallway to pick up their pace and race down the hall toward Busch's room.

Finn felt the slightest of tension around his hand when he heard a familiar voice in the hall. He was torn between turning around and seeing the face of his unit's C.O., which belonged to the voice, or clutching at any sign Joe would be waking up. When he felt the hand he was holding squeeze, let go, and then felt Joe squeeze once again, Finn's mind was made up. His unit's Commanding Officer, Captain Raul Hermosa, stood out in the hall being briefed by the guard still stationed outside. The Chief of Surgery was catching up on SGT Joseph Busch's status. Specialist Alan Finn was not going to leave his Sergeant's side.

Finn stared down at Joe. He was almost completely buried under tubes, wires, blankets, and bandages. Finn tried to mentally help Joe into opening an eye. Audrey stood there, paralyzed by what was happening in front of her eyes, and held a bloody washcloth.

It happened as subtlety as a butterfly kissing the back of a flower. It was almost as unnoticeable as one candle in a million others being snuffed out. When it finally and fully happened, it came like a lightning bolt. Joe opened one eye, winked, and then opened the other. He stared blindly at the ceiling feeling an irresistible urge to close his eyes against the blinding light above him and fall back in a peaceful sleep.

Joe wanted to go back to his dream, the dream he'd been envisioning and been haunted by for months. His prior interpretation was completely wrong. Joe wanted to go back and stand under his family's flag pole. He wanted to feel the absolute warmth and comfort he experienced when he pulled the tear-stained stars and stripes around his shoulders in the dream. He wanted to go home and tell his mother that "everything will be OK. I'm coming home, Mom."

Joe wanted to walk over to the strange sapling that was sown in the front yard of his life and touch its leaves. He wanted to peel back the strangely large bud that was growing on the topmost branch of the weak, little tree. He wanted to fall back to sleep and hope that this time he would be able to tell his girlfriend in his dream that he loved her with all his heart. That he wanted to marry her.

The strangest part, Joe thought to himself while squinting into the blinding light overhead, was that the fog swirling around his ankles seemed to pull at him stronger than he could ever remember. He wanted to know how that tornado snapped him out of his wondrous flight over the countryside occurred, without destroying all the crops and tearing him to pieces. He wanted to shout to the world over the crashing silence of his tears that he was coming home to be with everyone again. He wanted the world to know everything in his heart.

While he dozed off behind squinted eyes, he felt an extreme burning in his chest. It was worse than the last thing he remembered from the street. It burned as if a vile demon was rubbing a blowtorch against the inside of his left ribcage. It was trying horribly to force the searing flame through his armpit. It only got worse when the devil tried to talk to him. He remembered the old story that the devil will take on different shapes and voices to tempt someone to go against God's will.

The coy devil was taking on the shape of his soldier, Finn. Was he dead? Why should he listen to you? The devil had taken on the shape of his buddy. How Joe hated that. He was too smart for Joe. Lucifer had won. What did it matter? Joe was dead. He'd listen.

He turned his eyes on painfully sore muscles and tried to focus on the devil who talked to him. Wait. There was more than one. How could that be? One looks like Captain Hermosa. Finn was talking to him. He had changed shirts. Joe had to be dead. A mysterious man in the same type of shirt as Finn with a mask hanging around his neck, and... wow! The devil was hot to look at. Either that, or she was one spectacular angel. He heard Finn saying his name again and again.

Man, that boy is getting excited that I'm dead. He looks as if he is about to pop out of his skin. Fuck, my chest hurts! I thought I wasn't supposed to feel any physical pain when I died. Everything is muffled, too. Why?

"Joe, if you can hear me, you're alive," Finn said. "I need you to squeeze my hand to let me know you understand. Do you understand?"

Joe squeezed back. Finn's words were clearer than he ever remembered anything in the world. The pain in his chest climbed with every passing second. It was almost too painful to concentrate...to keep his eyes open. He knew if he could just close his eyes, the pain would stop. But he promised that he would be coming home. If he's dead or not, he still had to fight to get home and check out that new tree in the front yard.

He still focused on Finn. Then the stranger with the mask put a hand on his broad shoulder and leaned in to whisper something to him. They both kept looking at Joe and then at each other with Finn's face losing the excitement he had only a moment ago. Joe had been waking up. What had he been... yes...dead or alive?

Finn looked as if he were going to cry when the doctor finished speaking. The look in his eyes told Joe everything he needed to know. That man in the v-necked shirt told Finn something very bad about Joe.

Maybe he was dead? That might be the reason why Finn looked so sad. He had squeezed back, right? He did squeeze. He knew he had squeezed. Fuck it. Joe thought. Joe squeezed his right hand as hard as he could to fight for the only person holding his hand to know that he wasn't dead. He'd done this once before, and Finn believed him. Finn had seen him blink and kept him alive. Damnit, Finn. Look at me!

Joe squeezed and blinked. And blinked. He squeezed and blinked as hard as he could. God, he felt weak. He didn't know how much more fight he had in him. But that tree...he had to see what kind of tree it was.

Finn leaned over and closely looked Joe in his eyes.

Joe did his best to blink. There was a painful stinging surrounding his eyes. He squeezed and squeezed again. He could have sworn he felt a tear roll down his cheek.

"Sergeant, I..."

I'm here, Finn. Talk to me

"Sergeant, I know you can hear me. I can feel you squeezing my hand. I saw you blink, so I know you're in there somewhere...."

One more chance, Finn. Spill it. I am tired of fighting against this blowtorch in my chest.

"There's no easy way to say this, so I'll just say the bad news before the good news..."

There was good news? He just got shot and wanted to get home and see a cool, new tree. What kind of good news could there be that's cooler than that.

"Sergeant, you're paralyzed." Finn and the hot devil/angel cried together, "You're paralyzed from the chest down. Joe, I'm sorry, man."

What the? How come I can feel that torch in my chest? I am not paralyzed! I am not going to be a cripple! Joe wanted to scream at Finn for being such an asshole and telling a man who got shot that he was now a cripple. He wanted to scream that he'd rather be dead, really dead. Not just squeezing a hand and blinking, thinking he was dead. But actually, physically dead with no heartbeat and blood pooling in the bottom of his worthless body.

Joe tried to pull his hand away from Finn, but Finn held it close to his chest.

"Hang in there, Sergeant. I have some good news."

Finn stopped to look at the Captain, the man with the mask hanging from his neck, and the hot devil/angel now bawled uncontrollably.

"Sergeant, a Red Cross message was the only mail you had today. Remember you told me that you wanted your mail? Squeeze my hand if you remember?"

Joe squeezed and pleaded with Finn through his eyes to tell him the good news.

"You're going to be a father, Sergeant. You're going to be a daddy. We're going to get you home to that pretty girl you carry a picture of, and you're going to be a dad. Can you believe it?"

The torch in Joe's chest plunged into his gut. He wished he hadn't wished to be dead just a moment ago. He understood everything now. He knew why his Mom told him to come home in his dream. He knew the meaning behind the young sapling. He realized he was dead. The tornado was the Lord's way of telling him to hang on. That he would make it.

He didn't understand why God would paralyze him on the day he found out he would be a father. What kind of father can I be if I'm stuck in a wheelchair? Depending on a strap to hold me up? How can I live up to the proposal I sent to Sara? I can't even be a man to her. But I'm going to be a dad. I created life. I found this out just hours after I took lives. Joe thought about all this and turned his focus back to the blinding light on the ceiling above his bed. The sounds and lights all started to blend together and he closed his eyes. He cried.

He wanted to weep as loudly as he could, but no sound came out because of the tube in Joe's throat. Joe cried himself to sleep thanking God that he was a father and begging Him to end his life. He didn't want to be a father who couldn't be a dad or a husband. He didn't want to live anymore.

Sue lay quietly in bed next to Doug. Whimpering, she knew the dream was about to happen again.

The last two weeks passed like a haze for the community and family in New Vienna, Iowa. The news that SGT Busch lost his fight for life and was finally labeled as killed in action spread like a wildfire. It tore through the farms and homes, breaking hearts and rekindling memories of the young man when he was growing up. Sue and Doug couldn't go anywhere without seeing the yellow ribbons that the neighbors and town wrapped around their mailboxes and trees. Sue stopped answering the phone in the house. The well wishers and news reporters left their messages in a simple, black answering machine.

The obituary for her youngest son was printed on the day that Joe arrived home for the last time. His body arrived on a commuter jet into the Dubuque Regional Airport under the feet of commuters and travelers oblivious to the fact that a hero was aboard the aircraft in the cargo hold. Joe's family waited somberly in the airport for the passengers and their bags to exit the aircraft. Only after all the bags and suitcases were unloaded did the flight and ground crew give the green light for the local hero to be deboarded.

A platform that could be raised and lowered was brought and parked by the cargo hold of the jet. The hero's family waited by the giant, plate glass window to see their fallen son and brother. They dreaded the sight of the silver casket being unloaded. Without ceremony or fanfare, Joe arrived back in the Iowa summertime with the help of strangers. The ground crew slowly pulled him and his steel box out of the aircraft and onto the platform that would lower him to the ground. The hot, summer sun shone brightly on the polished silver casket. The strangers who rode with him to the hearse felt every bump in the tarmac on their silent ride to the black hearse.

When Joe was pulled out through the small cargo hold door in his final box, Sue and her family broke down. Doug tried to stand strong and be the man that time said the old farmer and father should be. A lone tear rolled down his cheek and landed in his wife's hair while he held her close, comforting her through their agony. He wanted to tear his eyes away from the nameless box that held his fallen son, but he couldn't. Doug forced himself to watch when the crew loaded his youngest son into the back of the hearse and shut the door. He watched, and the car drove away on the short trip back to town. There Joe would be dressed one last time in his finest uniform, the same from Sue's dream with the shiny jump wings and brass buttons. His maroon paratrooper beret would grace his head one last time in the under-taker's funeral home and fold his hands across his chest until doom's day.

Joe finally arrived back at his home in the heartland of America, keeping his promise that he swore he would when he left nine months before prior to Halloween.

Sue stared through the window of the white minivan when it passed the fields of corn that bordered either side of the highway. Row after row of green stalks of corn streaked behind her reflection on the window. Sue watched her reflection and tried to look herself in the eyes still red from crying after she had broken down once they had unloaded Joe from the airplane. Sue began to think again of the dreams and promises of youth that her son had had stolen.

She asked herself silently if Joe knew what love felt like and if he allowed his heart to be held by a woman. The thoughts of a mother grieving for her son who lost his battle only a month before his child's birth burst through her mind and flashed faster than the rows of crops went by. She hoped with all her heart that Joe experienced as much of life as possible in his short trip on this mortal coil.

Sue rested her forehead against the glass and clutched at a tissue in her hand. The afternoon sun blazed brilliantly and forced her to close her eyes. The images she witnessed behind her closed eyelids forced her to weep without a sound. She knew what it felt like to sit in a church and watch a child devote the rest of a life to another person. Her mind painted the picture of her son standing by the altar in St. Boniface Catholic Church with his best man and brothers at his side. The choir sang a song entitled "Be Not Afraid."

The hymn filled her ears and she raised her vision to the cross on top of the altar. She listened to how the song reminded the faithful not to be afraid. She imagined Joe's travels across a barren desert and speaking his words in foreign lands. He carried a message of freedom to the persecuted, and everyone understood. The choir raised their voices to the heavens above when they reached the part about Christ going before them always.

Sue's heart filled with sorrow, and she thought of Joe facing the terror in the night. She looked back to where Joe stood in the front of the church in her mind, only a moment ago. Joe smiled to her and his eyes thanked her for giving the life Sue gave to him. Even though she knew that this was impossible, Joe never looked happier than he seemed to be in her dream.

Without saying a word, Joe spoke silently to his mother while she rode without speaking. He told her not to worry, that he had lived his dreams. He told her about how he yearned to be in love and thought that he knew what love was. He told her through his eyes that his spirit would live on through her memories and his child would join the other grandchildren that would grow up to hear stories of an uncle and father who fought to give strangers hope.

Joe told her as the fields flew by that he would watch over his family in Iowa and that he would keep safe his Army brothers who still fought. Joe walked over to the pew in which Sue sat and leaned over *to take his mother's hand. He squeezed it tightly. He whispered to her heart that this dream in which he lived in her mind would never happen but thanked her for sharing in his dreams. He understood that it was time for him to go home.*

When he turned away, the choir in Sue's mind transitioned into another song. The sun shone through the stained glass windows, Sue's tears streaking down her cheeks when she recognized the song.

"Here I am, Lord. Is it I, Lord? I have heard you calling in the night. I will go Lord, if you lead me." The choir sang the simple words, their meaning profound.

Sue watched when her son walked to the side door of the church. The sun shining outside streamed like a river of light through the doorway as Joe opened the entrance to the church. His silhouette shattered into a blazing kaleidoscope of light when he stepped outside and the door slowly closed.

"BEEP...BEEP...BEEP!" Sue's alarm clock splintered the early morning silence. She woke up shaking from the nightmare that felt more real every time it appeared. She felt cold and rolled over to curl up next to Doug. Her arm fell on an empty spot in the bed, and Sue sat up and peered through the darkness trying to see where her husband was.

She spotted him standing by their bedroom window, dressed in his flannel, chore shirt and blue jeans, and sipping on a cup of coffee. He looked out the window at the dark and dew-covered fields.

"Come back to bed for a few minutes..."

"I haven't slept all night, Sue." Doug sipped his coffee. "I'm just not sure if I'm ready for this afternoon."

"It's going to be all right, Hon. He's coming home, and we gotta be strong for him and Sara. She's due next week," she said, pulling the covers up tighter around her while she sat in the middle of the bed.

"I just hope we thought of everything. We put the ramp in, converted the parlor into a bedroom for him, but that's not what I'm worried about."

"Let's just get through today, okay? It'll be tougher than anything we've ever done."

Doug finished the coffee and set the cup down on the night-stand next to the alarm clock. He sat down to put his work boots on. "I know, Honey. I know." Doug stepped into the worn-out leather boots and started to lace them up. "I heard you dreaming...same one?"

"Yeah. Same one." Sue felt it reappearing behind her eyes with that horrible coffin coming out of the plane.

Doug leaned back, laid his head in her lap, and looked up through the darkness. He saw the red light from the digital alarm clock reflecting off small streaks on his wife's cheeks before he said, "Honey, I love you. As much as I doubt that I'm prepared for this today, I know how strong you are. Everyone has drawn off your strength through the last months. You've only grown stronger through it all. It's going to be tough, but we have been through tough times during the last 35 years, haven't we?"

Sue thought through their years of marital bliss. Some years were less blissful than others, but she wouldn't change a thing. She grabbed Doug's stubbly chin and kissed him. "I love you."

"I love you, too," he swore and kissed her back with the passion and love that never faded.

"What about chores?" Sue asked.

"The cows can wait a few more minutes. This day will only get tougher as it goes on." He whispered and slipped out of his untied boots.

They lay together as one, tightly holding on to each other. Each offered the strength needed when they entered a new life providing for their son. He had paid more than could be counted in the hope that his child and their grandchildren wouldn't have to do what Joe had.

Chapter Twenty-Nine

Joe sat strapped into his seat, dressed in his sharply-pressed uniform. He stared through the window at the clouds just under the wings and thought about how this was eerily similar to the dream he had, just after being wounded. He looked down at his uniform making sure that everything was perfect. He double checked that his ribbons were straight, the silver jump wings centered above his rack, and his expert rifle badge placed perfectly underneath everything.

He had to get his uniform retailored at the end of his rehabilitation at Walter Reed Army Medical Hospital in Washington, D.C. None of his shirts fit, and his jacket hung loosely around his chest. He weighed twenty pounds less than the 205 when he was wounded. His chest had shriveled slightly with the absence of one entire lung. The ribs on his left side bore a small scar that covered a bumpy and rough set of healed ribs under his armpit. He hated the eight-inch-long scar that traced the center of his chest; the hideous thing was dotted with scars from the staples which the doctors had used to close his chest following his surgery.

Joe picked one leg up and held it for a second before putting it down and repeating with his other leg to keep the blood flowing. He looked around to make sure that no one was looking when he pinched his right leg as hard as he possibly could. Joe kept hoping that one time, just one time, he would feel the pinch. Joe did everything possible to hide the giant bruise he gave himself every time he pinched his legs, ashamed of the fact that he couldn't accept that he was paralyzed.

Joe thought back over the months of painful rehabilitation. He wished he would have swallowed his pride and asked Sara or someone from his family to come and join him or help him. Every time he looked into the mirror, he hated the way he looked. His body had shriveled, his legs were useless, and he couldn't feel any sensation in his groin. The catheter seemed to leak a lot and the atrocious smell made Joe hate himself more than ever.

He tried to write to Sara and answer her letters to him. He wanted to tell her how much her words kept him going and, honestly, kept him alive. He wished he could tell Sara how he was afraid of coming home. He could have been home months ago, doing treatment through a VA Outpatient Clinic, but he punched every mirror he looked into. He scarred his knuckles punching walls, mattress, and his legs trying to beat himself into walking, feeling, anything.

Joe didn't think anyone could love someone who needed help to get in and out of bed and couldn't perform as a man. "God hates me," Joe whispered to himself. "Hell, I hate me."

The plane shuddered as it rode out a wave of turbulence over the fields. The bouncing shattered Joe's wave of self-pity, and he flashed back to jump school and how scared he was just before his first ever jump. It was his first time ever taking off in an airplane. By the end of jump training, Joe had taken off in an aircraft five times without once landing. He leaned his head back against the headrest and wished that he could jump one more time.

Joe reached inside the lapel of his uniform jacket and pulled out a picture and folded note that was hastily written. The picture was a grainy black and white, barely showing anything more distinguishable than a large head with closed eyes. A tiny fist was raised to the small mouth while the fetus tried to suck on its thumb inside Sara's womb. He stared at the picture and stroked his thumb over the glossy finish.

"Hi, Baby. How are you? Still growing, I hope? Are you giving your Mom a hard time? I hope you keep reminding her about how much I loved, and still do, love her. Did you tell her our lil' secret, ehh kiddo? Who are we kidding? We could never keep a secret from her. I hope she hasn't given up on me. I know I haven't talked to her in a while."

Joe looked around the airplane. He was getting looks from the other passengers. Their eyes asked the questions they never would ask. They wanted to know why this soldier was dressed in his finest, with his maroon beret folded and draped over his dead legs. Why this man was holding a picture, talking to it, apologizing, and crying? Joe looked back at his child.

"I don't know how I can be a dad, kid. I know you will believe in me, but..." Joe tried to control his tears. "I don't know if I can do it. Trust me, I want to. I don't know if I can watch you grow up from in a chair. I don't want to look in your eyes and see pity. I don't know if I can stand to see your mother's eyes. I'm so afraid that it won't be love I see in the windows to her soul. I just don't know what I'm going to do if I all I see as I look around our families is pity. I love you, too. I gotta go before I lose it completely."

Joe wiped his eyes and left a damp mark on the sleeves of his uniform, but he didn't care. He put the picture back into the pocket over his heart and felt the other note he carried. It was the note that he got from the hospital in Baghdad, the one that his best friend Greg Forrester had written for Doug to read when his body got home. He carried that with him everywhere he went to remind him how close he came to being dead forever. Now he was just dead from the waist down.

"Sir, is there anything I can get for you?" the flight attendant asked.

Joe sniffled and said no thanks with as much pride as he could muster.

"Just to let you know, we'll be landing in about fifteen minutes, sir." She paused, wondering if she should continue. "There is a gentleman in the back who is also a veteran."

"Oh," Joe said almost disinterestedly.

"Umm, he wanted me to tell you that he lost an arm in Vietnam. He asked me to ask you if you would allow him to stay behind on the aircraft with you until it's time for you to deplane. He wants to walk with you and accompany you. He's really proud of you and says that he knows where you are right now."

A comforting blanket immediately surrounded and enveloped Joe. His half-empty chest filled with admiration and hopes that maybe his trip down the jet-way would be made a lot easier if he made the journey with another brother from the service. Hardly in control of his emotions, Joe softly spoke, "Can he come up and...sit with me before we land?"

The stewardess saw the welling of water in the Sergeant's eyes and comforted him with a hand on his shoulder. The thick, green jacket felt heavy under her fingertips, almost as if she slipped her fingers between a massive weight and his shoulder, which was tired from carrying it too long. "Of course. It would be my honor. Thank you for everything you have done, Sir."

Chapter Thirty

Dubuque Regional Airport
Thursday, July 17th, 2005, 10:25 AM:

Two families waited with signs and posters to wave at Joe to see when he came out of the jet way. Sara, heavily pregnant, paced back and forth in front of the plate glass windows, caressing her swollen belly. She could feel her active child kick and squirm while it ran out of room inside her. Pangs of indigestion swarmed over her from time to time, but she blocked them out and kept pacing and looking into the distance for an airplane to appear.

Doug and Sue sat together in uncomfortable airport chairs and watched their grandchildren play with their toys they had brought into the waiting area. Doug had to smile and chuckle when he saw Blake and Ben, two grandsons dressed in Army t-shirts, playing soldier around the rows of chairs. Sue clutched the beads of her rosary between her fingers. Joe's brothers and sisters stood or strolled around, constantly trying to keep their kids in line before they destroyed the area.

Sara stopped walking and pointed into the distance, "I think I see it."

The fellow veteran came up front and sat directly across the aisle from Joe. Before he buckled himself in for the landing, he stuck out his left arm. "I'm Mike. I served with the Marines in Vietnam."

"I'm Joe. Sergeant Joe Busch. How you doing, Mike?" He asked awkwardly shaking Mike's left hand and caught a glimpse of Mike's shirt sleeve pinned in place.

"Better now that I'm up here. How you holding up, son?"

"Nervous, not sure if I can do this."

"That's what I thought. I've been in your place, man. I've been exactly where you are right now."

"Thanks. That means a lot."

The camaraderie between the two servicemen sparked immediately. Both knew not to ask how their wounds happened. That part of their lives was over. There was no need to make the other talk about what was constantly playing in his mind.

"I heard you have an interesting picture."

"She told you about that?"

"Yeah. We sat and talked for a few minutes. Her dad was a Marine and veteran. She knows the look and picked me out."

"Oh!" Joe didn't know what to say.

"Can I see it?"

Joe reached into his pocket and pulled out the picture. He handed it to Mike, unable to look at the picture or Mike, too afraid that he would start crying again as the pilot began to bank the plane for approach.

"It's a snapshot of a miracle, Son," Mike commented while looking at the ultrasound picture. "I won't tell you how lucky you are because when I was sitting in your seat, I thought my life was over."

Joe sniffed back the salty emotions. "It is, though."

Mike put out his only arm across the aisle and squeezed Joe's arm. "It's tough, but this is the greatest gift God can give to you. It's your job now to be there and be the father this child needs."

"My baby needs a dad who can be a dad," Joe said softly, refusing to look Mike in the eye. "My baby's mother needs a man who can be a man for her. I can't do that from a chair," Joe answered and punched his legs with his weaker left arm. "Dead, man. Dead from the waist down."

Mike felt the tears starting inside his own heart as he stared at himself thirty years ago but forced them down. He knew the last thing this young soldier needed to see was pity. Mike clutched Joe's arm and told him, "That doesn't mean your heart is dead, man. Let me help you come home?"

Sergeant Joe Busch reached across his dead torso and grasped onto Mike's hand. "Thank you. I don't know if I can do it, but thank you, Sir."

The plane's landing gear touched down, and the pilot made a perfect landing unaware that just behind the cockpit two veterans held onto each other, helping the other to hang on.

Chapter Thirty-Two
Dubuque Regional Airport
Thursday, July 17th, 2005, 10:45 AM:

The scene went from amazing to chaotic. All the passengers left the plane and had gathered their bags before Joe had hung his arms around Mike's neck. He hung on as Mike stood and carried Joe to his chair outside the door of the aircraft. They were both crying for the prices they paid in service to their country. Joe asked if he would wait a second to gather himself before pushing him down the jet-way.

They waited together—Mike with his hand on the handle of the wheelchair that his younger service brother sat in and Joe taking apprehensive, excited, and scared breaths. "OK, Mike, let's do this."

Mike pushed Joe with more pride than he felt even after his only child was born. He wanted to tell Joe that when he came home, even with an arm missing, he would still be called a baby killer and rapist. This was just as important to Mike as it was to Joe while he helped him to a homecoming where cheers were filling the jet way while they rounded the corner and approached the door.

He rolled through the door, and Sara stood waiting for him, tears streaming down her cheeks, that familiar twinkle in her eyes. She ran to him and hugged him—her wet cheeks felt warm against his face. Joe tried to hold in his emotions and lost that battle without a fighting chance.

Joe broke down and cried while his family and Sara's surrounded him in his chair. He didn't want to ever let go of Sara, but he had to ask a question. He let go of his embrace and reached around his neck to unlock the loving hug. She backed up and asked, "What's wrong?"

"Did you get my letter?" he whispered and looked deep inside her eyes.

"I did, Honey. I did, I do, and I will." She fell to her knees and pulled his hands to hold hers. "I never took your ring off, and I never will. I never stopped loving you, and never will." She brought his hand down and placed it on their baby who was due in nine days.

Joe pulled her up and kissed her to cheers from both their families while his nieces and nephews hid behind their parents' legs making gross faces when they kissed. Joe cupped his hands under her face, "I love you, Babe. I love you so much."

They stayed like that, just looking at the faces they hadn't seen since they created the miracle inside Sara.

"Oh, my God!" Sara cried out, feeling an intense and wet warmth between her legs and running down her pantyhose, and her bout with indigestion took a severe turn on the pain scale.

"What is it, Babe?" Joe asked afraid that this was all a dream and he was just about to wake up back in the rehabilitation center.

Sara stood, backed away, and looked down. Her legs were completely soaked to her shoes. "I think my water just broke!"

"Now? Are you serious?"

She looked around at both their families with wonder and amazement and finally back to Joe, "Yeah, it did...are you ready to be a daddy?" She asked and leaned down to kiss him.

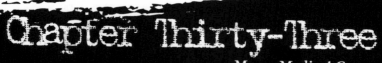

Chapter Thirty-Three

Mercy Medical Center
Friday, July 18th, 2005, 8:47 AM:
6:47 PM, 8 lbs, 14 oz. Nineteen and one-half inches long.

"He's beautiful, isn't he?" she asked, her hair sweat soaked.

"He's amazing," Joe said softly, surrounded by nurses and still holding the scissors he used to cut the umbilical cord.

"What should we name him?" Sara asked him.

"What do you want to name him?"

"I've had a few names in mind, but been leaning toward Joseph Henry Busch, Jr."

"It would be an honor. I love you, Sara." Joe started to roll away in his chair.

"Where are you going, Hon?"

"Someone's gotta tell the crowd outside." Joe hid behind a smile when he rolled through the double doors and into the hallway.

His emotions from the plane came boiling back with the force of a knife in his kidneys. His doubts about being a good father and a decent man flooded his mind. He kept having flashbacks to waking up in the Baghdad Hospital because of the bright lights inside the delivery room. Joe felt that he could never be the man that Sara deserved and needed in her life to help raise Joe, Jr.

Still in his dress uniform, but with the jacket hanging open, Joe wheeled himself into a corner of the hallway in the hospital to hide what he thought were selfish tears.

"I can't do this. I can't be what she needs," he sobbed to himself with his head hanging down. He saw the note that he carried with him throughout rehab sticking out of his pocket, and he reached in and pulled it out to read it again.

> *Doug and Sue,*
>
> *Doug, I don't know when or if you will get this note, but I needed to tell you several things about your son. I am finding it very hard to write this right now because Joe was killed only a few moments ago. I wish I didn't have to write this while kneeling next to him, but if I don't, I will not get the chance to see him again. I know that he is still with me right now helping me to write this letter and probably chuckling at some joke we always had between us. I wanted you to know that Joe was my best friend and brother. I know he talked a lot about me because I talked a lot about him. Doug and Sue, you raised a great man with a giant heart. He never failed to bring a smile to everyone's face.*
>
> *Doug, I want you to know that he died a hero. He saved my life only a few moments before by taking an enemy out that had the jump on me. Joe tried to fight as long as he could, and I am sure he knew that he wouldn't make it off this street because he never once asked for a medic. If it helps any, Joe passed quickly, and he looked very calm when I found him.*
>
> *Doug, I know that right now this is probably the hardest thing for you to read but Joe's memory will live on forever in the minds and hearts of the soldiers in this unit. I will never forget the bond between us. I apologize for crying while I write this note to you. I feel like I should have done more or run faster to find him, but even then, I am sure that he would have tried to tell me that he was all right. I pray that God watches over you and your family during this hard time. I know that there is a spot in heaven reserved for soldiers like your son. I have to go now, but I pray that these times pass quickly for you and that God blesses your family*

with many happy memories in the future. I will come and visit when I get home.

> *Sincerely,*
> *Greg Forrester*

Joe laid the letter down in his lap with his mind made up for what he had to do. He fumbled through a pocket on the side of his chair for the pen that he kept for emergencies.

Clicking it open, Joe poured his heart and soul out through a poem on the back of Greg's note about how he knew he couldn't go on living, feeling the way he did.

> *Dear Mom,*
> *Dear Dad,*
> *I know*
> *that I have not*
> *written in awhile.*
>
> *I am*
> *sorry*
> *that you*
> *have to find out*
> *in such a way.*
>
> *I never*
> *thought that*
> *it would*
> *come to this kind*
> *of terrible end.*
>
> *You are*
> *the best*
> *parents*

that a kid could
be raised by.

I want
you to
know that
you have nothing
to do with this.

This was
my choice,
my way,
out of my hell
and this tells all.

Selfish,
childish,
young,
probably all wrong
in your wise eyes.

But to
me, it
was the
final end to
my internal pain.

I know
I have
failed,
as a son, and
as a man to Sara.

Jacob Lawrence Krapfl

I failed
my men.
their deaths,
their blood, will not
wash from my hands.

I think
back to
the order,
that fateful order,
that almost killed me.

It haunts
my dreams
at night,
I wish that I
could have died.

The pain
is too
much to
bear by myself.
now I must go.

By my
own hand,
my own
weapon will take
the life you gave.

I hate
to say
goodbye,

but the time has
drawn near to my end

My family,
my men,
my Sara,
please forgive me,
as I take what
is not mine to take.

I hope
to see
you all
on the other side.
forgive me...please.

Joe took the back hallway away from the waiting room and came out by the emergency room's front desk. He pulled up and punched the bell, barely able to see over the countertop.

"Can you page Doug Busch in fifteen minutes, Ma'am?"

The nurse looked at him with a puzzled look. "Why?"

"I have to go outside for a smoke and get to another appointment, but he'll want this note." Joe held up the note for her to see. "Can you do this for me?"

"Yeah, I guess I can." The nurse shot him a dirty look for mentioning that he smoked.

"Thank you, Ma'am." Joe spun the chair around and started rolling out the door.

"You know that'll kill you," she hollered in a self righteous tone while he waited for the doors to open.

"I'm already dead." Joe rolled out into the sunset outside the hospital.

Three weeks later, on August 2nd, the sheriff's department pulled Sergeant Joe Busch's wheelchair from the Mississippi River.

The day that Sue's son was put into the ground inside an empty casket arrived in a spectacular manner. It was as though Mother Nature lost one of her sons, and this was her way of grieving. The sun rose in a glorious mix of pinks and blues and yellows that highlighted the fluffy, cumulous clouds in the Iowa morning sky. Even the cattle that Doug milked that morning must have known something was amiss.

The memories from the Funeral Mass in St. Boniface Catholic Church in New Vienna were hazed over with sad memories and tears that were shed by everyone attending. Sue remembered the music was beautiful and sad. Daniel delivered the eulogy about the last Christmas the family spent with the town's fallen hero. He closed the remembrance speech with the last words he spoke to his little brother.

"Joe, I said to you last time I saw you to make sure you came back home so we could have someone to talk about during deer season." He sobbed, trying to hold back the tears. "But don't worry, little brother. We will remember you this season and every season to come. Everyone will miss you, not only in the woods with your happy, trigger finger but also every day of our lives. You made this world a better place. I wish I could have spent more time with you, but I know that you're in a better place and looking down upon us from the spot in heaven reserved for fallen soldiers. I just want you to know that we will see each other again someday." Daniel did not know if he could go on without completely breaking down. He found the courage to tell his courageous fallen brother one more sentiment. "Joe, we love you and miss you. Stop in from time to time and check on us and keep us safe. We will light our paths with your example, and may God never put another... family, through...this... pain again."

Joe's casket was laid to rest in the cemetery next to the church. His plot was next to his grandparents near the center of the cemetery. The flag that draped his coffin was folded and presented to a weeping mother under the hot, summer sun. Sue and Doug remember hearing the shots from his twenty-one gun salute by the VFW signaling Joe's death and burial. The folded flag felt heavy in her hands after she accepted it from the same Army soldier who had brought them the news that Joe was wounded in combat. The three polished brass rounds that were tucked into the folds of the flag represented the three volleys of shots from the local veterans honoring their fallen brother.

Sue's mind recalled the ending of her dream when Joe slipped below the grass line into his resting place. She smiled up into the sun while the scene played out one last time in her mind. Joe was standing under the flagpole outside their home in the countryside with the stars and stripes clutched to his breast. "I love you, Mom, and I will see you again someday." His voice echoed in her mind.

"I love you, too, Joe." She cried when their families and friends around her finished the Lord's Prayer.

"Forgive us our trespasses, as we forgive those who trespass against us," they prayed, "And lead us not into temptation, but deliver us from evil."

Sue cried out for the last time through her tears and broken heart, "I love you so much."

"For thine is the kingdom, the power, the glory, now and forever."

"Amen." Sue whispered, "Amen."

Afterword

Dear Readers,

The story you have just read is a fictional story which I wrote while I was in counseling for my own PTSD and brush with suicide. The following is some of the truth surrounding the infinitesimally complex problem of veteran suicide. It is also the story of how I took my first step away from the edge.

We cannot expect to stumble upon a solution to prevent all veteran suicides, but together we can change a few things in our communities. We can begin by shining a light into the shadows cast by war onto the lives of all veterans and their families. Together, we can.

Sincerely,
Jacob Lawrence Krapfl

August Destiny

It was a hot, sticky August night in 2007 when he made the call.

His note was written, and it sat on his kitchen table waiting to be found. He had been out of the service for thirteen months, just trying to make it on his own, but in his mind, he was failing miserably. He had his mind made up that he couldn't deal with it any longer, and this was his last and only call for help. If no one answered, the note would be all that he had left behind.

"Veterans Affairs, Iowa City. How may I direct your call?"

He hesitated, afraid of what the stranger on the end of the line would think of a soldier admitting something was wrong with his mind. "I can't take it any longer, ma'am. I don't think I can go on..."

Every day in America, 18 veterans commit suicide.

"Sir, do you feel like you want to hurt yourself or someone else?"

He could barely squeak out, "No one else, just myself."

The cigarette between his lips quivered, unlit. The young man cried in the darkness, and he didn't even know he was crying. The voice in his ear kept telling him over and over that "everything is going to be OK. Just hold on a few more minutes, Sir and we'll get someone on the line to listen. Just know that you're not alone anymore, buddy. You're not alone anymore."

He lit the cigarette, and took the first breath of his new life. A survivor.

He made it through the night, and was sitting in a psychologist's office at the Iowa City VA hospital the next day.

It was on that hot, sticky day in August when I was that man. I stood on the edge of that suicidal cliff where soldiers complete the enemy's mission. I thought I was alone, but I was surrounded by my brothers and sisters in arms. None of us knew the others were there in the darkness. We'll never know how many get to the edge and back away, but we know how many don't back away.

We can do something about those eighteen, but first we have to understand who they are, what pushed them to the edge, and most importantly...why.

These are men and women in our communities who have answered our nation's call to service. These are our neighbors and friends whom we barbecue with and watch the fireworks in July next to, but we turn a blind eye when we see that they stare at the ground throughout the explosions and echoes.

According to the VA's National Center for Post-Traumatic Stress Disorder, 30% of Vietnam veterans have PTSD and 10% of Gulf War vets. The numbers coming out of the current War on Terror estimate 11-20% of veterans coming home from Afghanistan and Iraq are developing PTSD. But, because of a stigma that's attached to having a mental illness, less than half of the total number, which is somewhere between that 11-20% and the total number of veterans, that need help are actually getting that help.

...afraid of what the stranger on the end of the line would think of a soldier admitting something was wrong with his mind. "I can't take it any longer, ma'am. I don't think I can go on..."

It's this fear that pushes some of our vets to the edge of that cliff. The fear of what our communities will think when they find out that the veteran who doesn't like to talk about the war has a mental health issue. An Operation Enduring Freedom Vet who spent 15 months in Afghanistan said, "People assume that you are going to go on some kind of killing rampage, and that you are so mentally unstable that your decisions are not sound."

This is not true, and this is the stigma that every person has a duty to fight. After all, we don't go up to someone with Tourette's Syndrome and ask when the next twitch is going to happen...

We have to start asking ourselves why veterans, as a group which only makes up about 10% of the population, are committing almost 20% of the suicides. What is even more alarming is a fact which the New York Times addressed on February 5, 2009, concerning one branch of our military's active duty during just one month. "The number of soldiers who committed suicide in January could reach 24, a count that would be the highest monthly total since the Army began tabulating suicides in 1980." That is more than the Army lost in combat to enemy fire in the same month.

I know that some of my readers will think we can approach this problem as though it were just a problem more prevalent in the larger society, as though vets were no different, psychologically speaking. I am not a psychologist, and I don't know of too many vets that read psychological diagnoses handbooks for pleasure, but veterans are not psychologically the same as the rest of the population.

Even the men and women, whom I've talked to, who were able to smoothly transition out of the military lifestyle openly admit that something is different about how we think. A corrections officer with two tours in Iraq, a fifteen month tour in Afghanistan, and a Purple Heart on his chest says what made it easiest for him to transition out was picking a civilian career in which a lot of his coworkers had military histories.

What about the ones who are not able to surrounded themselves with prior military servicemen and women?

"I think," An Operation Enduring Freedom Vet says. "that being built up mentally and physically and then when returning to civilian life…most of what they believed to be their strong attributes [will not] transfer over to the political systems of advancement in civilian life. Structure can breed institutionalization and breaking that feeling of needing ones brothers in arms is hard to get over."

When we get to that edge, we feel like we're alone. We know that our brothers are out there, but we've been cut off in the darkness. It's kind of like sitting in a guard tower, and your buddy and you have passed the point of talking; you just stare out into the glow of the hostile city that surrounds you. You know that if you fall asleep, you could get someone killed. So you try not to. You make the radio checks with command. And you see that your buddy is falling asleep. Do you let him sleep, and you'll just watch twice as hard?

No, you give him one of your smokes, and get him to start talking while you listen.

Society has fallen asleep while our vets are bringing the nights in the towers home with them. We're getting tired of watching twice as hard while everyone else sleeps and this is beginning to be seen across the country. A veteran at the University of Iowa said "I feel people judge me on the actions I have taken in my life, and I don't volunteer information about the service to my classes and almost try to avoid telling them I served; not that I am embarrassed, just that I don't want to answer all the subsequent questions." He is tired of waking others up, and he has resigned himself to keep what he has seen to himself.

A female National Guard service member told me about some of the troubles I previously thought only happened on active duty. "Over a third of our battalion went through divorces as just a start. We didn't have the knowledge of how to prepare our lives for when we returned. When I left, I had two and a half years in college, two jobs, good credit, was engaged, had my own vehicle, place to live, etc. When I returned, my relationship was over. My vehicle and credit ruined. I was living with my parents for the first time since I was 18. I didn't get reemployed by either job (one being the city and the military stepped in); life as I knew it was gone and I didn't know how to adapt."

One of the common misconceptions that accompanies this stigma of servicemen and women affects them regardless of their mental health. When others find out that we are vets, we are expected to be cold and emotionless. This is also extremely troubling because it is us who have explored the depths and range of our emotions under extreme circumstances. Sometimes, the only thing that gets us through the days is what gets a veteran through the toughest of times, hope.

That same female National Guard member, who served her tour in the opening days of the Iraq war shared her experience, and where she found her hope. "I had a VERY difficult time when I came back in 04...in fact; I basically crashed for 3 years. I didn't care about me or anything else. I had no goals anymore, slept through up to 8 days with hyper-somnia and severe depression...it was bad. If I didn't get pregnant with my daughter, I could have been a statistic just as easily. Now I have refocused and have a whole new meaning to life."

I asked the Veteran from the University of Iowa what he feels when he tells someone he was a soldier, and they take it upon themselves to tell this veteran what he did wrong throughout his service. "I do feel a loss of pride in my country when people bash on those men and women serving in the armed forces." Does he hope any longer for our generation?

"I hope that future generations look back on those of us who are living breathing patriots and realize the sacrifices that we made to support our country."

A fellow veteran, who found hope in her new child, talks about the extremely unique experience of combat veterans. "They are willing to give everything up for the good of all. Even if it isn't their physical body that is taken by the war, it may still be their life..."

Days come and go for him now. Some better than others. The doctors told him that he'll never be cured of PTSD; all he can "hope" for is to learn coping mechanisms. He still wakes up in the middle of the night, and he hasn't watched the fireworks in years. There's one day out of the year when he pulls that note out, November 8th; the day when a rocket propelled grenade missed him by three feet.

In his letter to his parents, he had written "my own hand will take the life you gave. My family, my men, please forgive me, as I take what is not mine to take. I hope to see you all on the other side. Forgive me...please."

Even though he still has ten fingers and ten toes, he knows because he's counted to make sure the dream wasn't real, part of him died fighting his battle with PTSD, alone and cut off from his men. He can't put that part of him to rest until he lays down for his final time, but every day he thinks about how close he came to taking what wasn't his to take.

His buddy tells him, "Those actions that we had to take to secure our safety and to complete the missions...have changed us, but we are what Americans should be."

It was a hot, sticky night in August when a stranger talked me back from the cliff. A Guardswoman discovered hope in her child. She had a little girl, whom I have never met, but I am willing to bet that little girl is as beautiful as her name. Destiny.

If you know or suspect someone who is thinking about hurting themselves, please do not hesitate to call
1.800.273.TALK

5281614R0

Made in the USA
Lexington, KY
24 April 2010